ACKNOWLEDGMENTS

Many thanks to the people who helped me with *Lockstep*, especially the wonderful professionals at Reedsy: Nick Castle who designed the cover and Katherine Sands for her developmental edit.

Most of all, a thousand thanks to my Launch Team for your support. You guy's rock!! I would like especially to thank the following members of the team whose eagle eyes found lots of errors missed by the proofreader and corrected some of the errors I made. They are, alphabetically: Andrew Stewart, April W. Vivas, Beverley Canuel, Cindy Warrick, Debbie Francis, Diane Griffin, Gayle Siebert, Gina Hines, Holly Stolarski, Janet Cline, Kathy Bockus, Linda Harbour, Lisa Mauk, Lorraine Garant, Mary Roberts, Melissa Ann Sanchez, Paula Cope, Pauline Burke, Rick Connolly, Sherry Jenkinson, Shirley Blane, Sue Ann Kelly and Tony Montague. I am sorry if I missed anyone.

As always, I would also like to thank the Vancouver Public Library for providing the perfect working location for any writer. Every word of *Lockstep* was written here.

To my wonderful wife Penny who believed in me when I had stopped believing in myself.

ALSO BY ROBERT P. FRENCH

Junkie (Cal Rogan Mysteries Book 1)

Oboe (Cal Rogan Mysteries Book 2)

COMING SOON

Three (Cal Rogan Mysteries Book 4)

1

CAL

WEDNESDAY

The wound must be bleeding heavily and hurts like hell. It's definitely slowing me down, just when I need to be fast. I know the smell of blood will be easy for the dogs to track and will excite them mightily.

As if in reminder, I hear the baying again. How far behind me are they now? Less than half a mile?

In the growing darkness beneath the forest canopy, I can hardly see the branches and brambles. They're snatching at my clothing and at the heavy pack on my back, slowing me even more.

For an instant the distraction of my wound has caused my focus to waver from its prime task of navigation. Have I lost the path? If I have, I'm dead meat. Literally.

Hell! I think I have. I feel the hand of panic tearing at me.

I slow and check the left side of the trail carefully.

No, I'm OK.

What a relief! There's the pine with the broken branch and the notch cut from its trunk: my first marker.

I turn and run into the bush to the left of the trail.

Crashing through the undergrowth, the waves of guilt flood through me again.

I suppress them. I had no choice… or so I tell myself.

No time to think.

I emerge onto a narrow trail leading south and place all my attention on avoiding the many exposed roots. I count them with care. I have to. My life depends on it.

I successfully navigate the first five. Now the greatest hazard of all. If I did this right only to screw it up now, I am in for a world of hurt. Maybe even death, which, given the circumstances, might be preferable.

I stop and listen.

Above the noise of the dogs comes a voice shouting a guttural command. The guards will miss my move from the main trail but the dogs won't. I look back and can see erratic motions of flashlights carried by the running guards. I remove the tiny Maglite from the pocket of my pants and point it on the ground to the right of the trail.

My skin crawls and I can feel the hair standing up on the back of my neck. One mistake now and… but no, there it is, the innocuous broken stick lying casually across a growth of those tiny blue forest flowers that bloom everywhere in the spring: my second marker.

I scan the air above the stick and wave my Maglite at belly height. My heart is in my throat. It's gone… No, wait a minute, there it is. I reach out and my trembling hand comes into contact with it. It is better concealed than I thought. Good. My pursuers will have their eyes and their flashlights trained on the path, looking for the next recalcitrant root. They will not see the thin filament, coated in non-reflective black dye, exactly three feet above the path.

I drop carefully to my knees and then, on my belly, scramble forward. Although all logic tells me that the wire is at least twelve inches above my backpack, my skin crawls as I pass underneath it. I grunt at the pain caused to my wound. When I am sure I am at least six feet past, I stand and, spurred on by the sound of more frenzied barking, I continue along the path at a steady jog. I am sweating freely in the cool spring-like air.

Suddenly, I am through the woods and running—or would hobbling be a better description?—down the green-clad slope leading to the pebble beach. I am both relieved and anxious at the same time. Relieved at being so close to the boat and anxious that I am now in the open, vulnerable to both eyes and bullets.

In the dim dusk I can see the two patches of reeds, the larger of which conceals the boat.

A resurgence of baying—it sounds closer and I pray that the guards have not yet let slip the dogs of war, for if they have, I will likely be torn apart—forces me to sprint the last one hundred yards to the beach. God only knows what it's doing to the wound in my side.

I reach the water's edge and now time, as lawyers like to say, is of the essence.

The pack is off my back even before I stop running and with two quick snaps the top is open and I am pulling out the drysuit.

I deviate from the carefully rehearsed sequence and pull up my black polypropylene turtleneck. At the back where the bullet entered, the hastily applied duct tape has stanched the flow but the exit wound at the front, four inches to the left of my navel, has blood seeping ominously around the tape.

I know I have to take precious time to deal with the bleeding.

I remove my gloves and from a side pocket in my pack, I pull out a Ziploc bag containing alcohol-soaked gauze pads and a roll of duct tape, there at the insistence of Stammo.

I suppress a cry of pain as I wrench off the existing tape, the pain from the wound itself and from the hundreds of hairs that are ripped from their follicles. The sight of the wound is horrific, made much more so by the fact that it is in my gut. Blood is flowing freely.

The baying is closer. Can they smell my blood?

How the hell did I get into this?

CAL

MONDAY EVENING, 9 DAYS EARLIER.

I scan the crowd, looking for a face. It may be a face I already know. It may not be; it may just have the look, the look I learned to recognize in my almost thirteen years as a cop in the Vancouver Police Department.

I am standing on the back corner of the makeshift stage in the gymnasium. The candidate is not yet in evidence. People are still streaming in through the two sets of double doors and planting themselves on folding chairs. I cannot tell if they will be friendly or hostile.

They are a mixed bunch. The majority are local activists and some of the neighborhood's better-off minority. There are a couple of well-dressed businessmen and quite a few homeless or near-homeless. Most are residents of Strathcona, V6A: Canada's poorest postcode. It was my home for much of the time I lived on the streets.

My eyes land on three young men with hard eyes. Their clothes are worn and old. Their physical ticks give away their addiction to crack. Anger is written into their faces. The security team may need to deal with them and though they are not my number one concern, I put them on my mental list.

Through the doors walk a couple with a baby. It is tiny,

swaddled. They don't make their way immediately to the seats but instead take in the details of the room. They look toward the makeshift stage with its podium and for a moment the man's eyes connect with mine, we nod and smile at each other. The wife's eyes scan the room. She speaks to her husband and gestures toward the back of the gym, farthest from the stage and close to where the only other doors are located. He nods and they make their way back there taking the two seats closest to the back door, a precaution against the baby crying: the mother can make a quick exit with a minimum of disturbance.

I take them off my mental list but add a man in a coat which is just a bit too baggy. He makes his way to a seat, stage left. My eyes drill into him as he sits. I look for any awkward movements that might give away the presence of a weapon concealed under the baggy folds. Looks OK but I keep him on the list with the hard-looking crackheads.

I scan the faces of people coming through the doors and see a face I know.

Goliath. A reminder of the past I can't escape. A member of a drug gang, arrested by the VPD as the result of my investigation into the murder of my best friend. He is a giant of a man, walking with a limp. If he sees my face, he will remember me as the man responsible for that limp and he will almost certainly come after me. I step off the back of the stage and partially conceal myself behind the backdrop; I don't want my past to create waves for the candidate. I scan my memory for Goliath's real name. It's Guy Chang. I am surprised he's out of prison so soon. He looks around the room at the crowd and then makes his way to the back. He sits a few seats away from the couple with the baby, multiplying my worry index. If he is here for some nefarious reason, I don't want that baby put at risk.

The room slowly fills up. There are a lot of people here to listen to Larry Corliss speak. He was popular in this community when he was Mayor of Vancouver and all the polls say he will win the upcoming Federal election against incumbent Edward Perot.

There is a buzz in my ear.

"Five minutes, Rogan," a voice says. "Any suspects?"

I raise my left hand and scratch my hair at the temple so that I can talk unobtrusively into my sleeve. "Yes three." I say, feeling like a member of the US Secret Service's Presidential Detail.

"To the door." It is not a request.

I step off the side of the stage and taking care not to trip over any feet, I take the narrow isle in front of the first line of chairs. I keep my head turned so Goliath won't catch a look at my face. Four hard-looking men are waiting for me at the doors. They work for the security company controlled by Arnold Young, my biggest client.

I point out the man in the baggy coat and the crackheads. Two of the guards go off to sit beside them.

Flanked by the other two security guards, I leave through the main doors, walk down the corridor beside the gym and re-enter in silence via the back doors. We stand, quiet and unnoticed, behind Goliath and the couple with the baby.

The man on my right is Ian Peake; we've met before. Ian once provided a protection detail for my daughter and her grandparents. He is a former sergeant in the British SAS. Enough said. He and his colleague are among the few civilians in Canada licensed to carry concealed weapons in public, our gun laws being one of the reasons that the country only has about two hundred gun homicides a year and most of those are gang members thinning each other's ranks.

The background murmur of the crowd changes its tone and a few people stand up and cheer as Larry Corliss enters the room followed by two of Ian's cohort. Two VPD patrol officers—one male, one female—walk in and stand beside the stage. I notice the man in the baggy coat, on the other side of the room, is also standing but he is not clapping or cheering. The security guard sitting beside him also gets to his feet and starts clapping. It's a smart move. His arms are already in motion; if the guy tries something, he can redirect his movements quickly.

Consummate politician that he is, Corliss stands and waves at the crowd, acknowledging a few individuals with points and smiles. I can feel his charisma from where I'm standing.

I look at Goliath. He is not standing nor does he look in the direction of the man in the baggy coat.

Having milked it as much as he can, Corliss signals for people to sit down. He moves behind the podium. Although no one would know, it is bulletproof and provides a modicum of protection from the chest down. Speaking without notes, he starts his speech and the opening words are the reason for all this security.

"Ladies and Gentlemen, the *only* people who benefit from the war on drugs…" he pauses, "are the drug dealers."

His opening line elicits a cheer from the audience. Covered by the noise, Ian and his colleague move a step closer to Goliath.

I hear the door behind me open.

The back door. The door that should be restricted to security personnel.

I spin around to see four men in suits coming through. I scan their faces. No one familiar. Not one of them radiates the hard look. They have smiling, placid, pudgy faces.

One of them points to a group of empty seats and they make their way to them.

Ian and I exchange glances. He shrugs.

The woman with the baby has turned at the noise of the opening door and is looking at me. I smile and she smiles back.

"No matter what laws we may enact," continues Corliss,

"people are going to use drugs. Some of them are going to get addicted and are going to spend whatever it takes to feed their habits."

A baby cries.

It's the baby of the couple in front of us.

It cries again and the mother rocks in her seat. She whispers something to her husband.

I look at Ian. He smiles and shakes his head.

We focus our attention on Goliath and on the man in the baggy coat.

Corliss' voice has gone up a decibel or two, "An addict willingly pays ten bucks for one tenth of a gram of heroin. Heroin that costs less than three thousand dollars a kilo to harvest and manufacture." The baby cries again, as if in protest, and a few members of the audience chuckle.

"The ninety-seven-thousand-dollar profit on that kilo of heroin ends up, tax free, in the pockets of the worst criminals this planet has ever known."

The baby wails and Corliss smiles and nods. "Yes, I know," he says. "It makes me cry too."

Amid the audience's laughter, the parents stand. The mother looks embarrassed but the father's face is inscrutable.

They make their way down the side aisle toward the entry doors. I had assumed they sat at the back of the gym so they could slip out through the rear doors.

Why aren't they?

I cut a glance at Goliath. He is focused intently on them. There is a tension in his body, like a cat waiting to pounce.

"It's them, the couple with the baby." I hiss into Ian's ear.

He's a pro. He doesn't question. He doesn't even look at me. He moves fast down the aisle toward the couple, his colleague in his wake. His left arm moves up to his face and his words come through my earpiece.

"Targets. Couple with baby, approaching doors."

The two uniforms beside the stage move fast to the doors.

Out of the corner of my eye I see the security guard on the other side of the room yank his neighbor to his feet and strip the baggy coat off him but there are no weapons in evidence. The other guard is focused on the crackheads.

The couple sees the police officers converging on them. After a moment's hesitation, the man reaches for the bundled baby in the woman's arms but Ian is right there; with one flowing movement, he takes the man down.

His colleague heads for the woman. She takes one look and turns back toward the doors. She'll take her chances with the uniforms.

The female officer is faster and reaches the doors first.

The audience realizes something is up. Corliss has stopped in mid-sentence and a murmur runs through the crowd.

The woman runs toward the officer and tosses the swaddled baby into the air in her direction. The audience gasps. The baby is just cover, it's not real, but if the officer suspects this, she doesn't take the chance. She takes two steps back and catches the swaddled bundle like she plays for the BC Lions.

The woman hurtles into the crash bar of the closest door, just as Ian's colleague grabs her coat collar and yanks her off her feet.

In less than five seconds from my hissing into Ian's ear, it's all over.

Except that it's not.

I turn toward Goliath.

He is on his feet and heading toward the rear door. Our eyes meet and his widen in recognition. Hatred suffuses his face.

As I move to cut him off, his right hand snakes around behind him.

I am unarmed. I only have one option.

I explode toward him and shout the warning: "Gun!" Just in case.

He steps away as he tries to wrestle his weapon out of his waistband but backs into a chair and is off balance when I crash into him. He goes over backwards and hits the floor with me on top. I can smell garlic and fish in the whoosh of breath from his lungs.

Hoping that his right hand is trapped underneath him—and if it isn't, that his weapon is not a knife—I arch backwards and drive my forehead hard into his nose.

As I roll off Goliath and spring to my feet, I recognize the ribbed barrel of a Heckler and Koch SPF9 in his tattooed hand. However my 'Liverpool kiss' has left him blinded, but only for a few seconds.

Around us, pandemonium reigns. The audience was bemused by the action at the main doors but the open violence mixed with my shouted warning has people running for the exits. As I raise my foot to stomp on the hand holding the gun, an elderly man pushes past me; I nearly lose my balance, step back and trip over a fallen chair.

With amazing agility for such a large man, Goliath is on his feet and is wiping the tears from his eyes. He sees me and levels his gun at my chest. I am transfixed. I feel a tightening in my chest and a loosening in my bowels. The best I can hope for is to get out of this with just a wound.

Then he grins, savoring the moment. "Good bye, Rogan," he says, the smile broadening. "This is a little present from—"

The sound of his body hitting the back wall is overwhelmed by the sound of the gun that shot him. The H & K flies out of a nerveless hand.

I haul myself to my feet hoping I'm not shaking visibly, Ian runs over, gun no longer in view. He kneels beside Goliath. The latter is moaning, his left hand clamped over his right shoulder. The male police officer comes and kneels on the other side of him. None too gently, the officer handcuffs him and then uses his radio to request backup and an ambulance.

I look around the gym. The audience has disappeared. I walk over to the main doors. The 'couple' is handcuffed and the baby's swaddling has been unraveled to reveal an Uzi and an old-fashioned cassette tape recorder.

I feel a touch on my shoulder.

"Thank you, Cal." Larry Corliss extends his hand.

I take it. "My pleasure, Mr. Mayor." I use his former title out of habit.

He smiles for a moment.

"They're serious, aren't they?" he says.

"Yes, sir, they are."

"Did you know that since I declared my candidacy for this constituency and announced I would build my platform on the legalization of drugs, I've received quite a few threats?"

"I'm not surprised, sir."

"I just never thought they'd…" He sighs. "Well, I guess this town hall meeting is over."

"I'm sorry it was so short," I say.

He half smiles. "Don't worry. When life hands you lemons, make lemonade. I'll make the late TV news and it will be in all the morning papers. Also, I can use this incident on Wednesday in the debate."

He walks off and I wonder if next time the assassins will be more efficient.

3

CAL

I am trembling. Is it from my body's reaction to the wound or my mind's reaction to the closeness of the dogs?

Gritting my teeth, I fold the tatters of skin and flesh over the wound and, with my left hand, press three large gauze pads on the area, unable to suppress the gasp at the sting of the alcohol. Using my right hand, teeth and bloody hunting knife, I tear off four strips of the silver duct tape with which I secure the gauze tightly over the wound. Two more pieces and the gauze is invisible under the tape. That will have to do; there is no time for further ministrations.

I pull on the dry suit and fasten it except for the hood; I still need my ears free. I slip the strap behind my neck and pull the mask forward on to my forehead. The dry suit immediately makes me feel hot. This is good; in a moment I will need all the warmth it can provide.

Quickly checking that I've left nothing on the ground, I swing my pack onto my left shoulder and wade into the patch of reeds.

I break several of the reeds in the process. I want it to be obvious that this is where I entered.

13

The reeds, so rare in west coast waters, are thick and strong. They grow to as high as six feet above the surface of the bay and their concealment gives me a momentary sense of security.

As I wade through the reeds, I hear the almost continuous sounds of the dogs, they know their quarry is close and are being encouraged by the shouts of their handlers.

Then loud cursing from two of the voices and, although I cannot make out the Spanish words, I am quite sure one of them has tripped on the clutching hand of a root and one of his companions has fallen on top of him. Despite the dire circumstances, I can't help but smile and be grateful that this experience will ensure their eyes stay focused downwards.

With a sudden chill, I realize that in his tumble, the guard may have dropped the leash of his dog, freeing the beast to run ahead and pass free under my booby-trap wire, or worse, trip it early.

I suppress the thought and press on through the reeds, which are starting to thin. They allow me to peer through them until I see my target, the sturdy aluminum dinghy with its powerful outboard motor. I smile at the silent figure seated in the stern.

Manny sits motionless, dressed as I am under the drysuit: black shirt, pants and woolen hat; he has been in position, waiting, for twenty hours. His blue eyes stare fixedly at the prow of the dinghy; his hand is on the tiller of the outboard motor. Manny will not let me down.

A barking dog is very close, I imagine him standing and slavering on the edge of the shore, undecided on his course of action. Whether or not my imagination is correct, I don't know. Then he makes his decision. I hear a splash as he launches himself into the water and starts to paddle his way through the reeds, alternating gasps of breath with grunted barks.

Because we knew there were dogs, I have a can of pepper

spray, bought from the camping supply store. The owner was a red-faced man with a drinker's nose and the most luxuriant mustache that I have ever encountered. He guaranteed me that the spray would deter even a grizzly bear. I silently promise myself that if his advice proves false, I will track him down and remove that magnificent facial hair strand by strand by strand.

Assuming I live.

But I have to live, for Sam and Ellie.

I reach down to my left pocket where I keep the spray can, except that of course, it is in my pants pocket under the dry suit.

In a panic, I unzip the suit, being careful to keep the zipper above the surface of the water, which is up to my waist. Awkwardly, I slide my left hand inside the suit and fumble in my pants pocket. My hand is encased in a rubber glove which is part of the dry suit and try as I might I cannot pull it and the spray can out of the pocket. In a flash of irrelevance, I think of the monkey unable to pull his hand from the glass jar while it is clutched firmly around the apple.

This thought vanishes as I glimpse the dog, mere feet away, paddling steadily through the reeds toward me.

Up close, he is smaller than expected but somehow more fearsome. Chestnut brown with a white patch over his left eye, his head is wide and square like a pit bull, his mouth open in a rictus of determination and, now that his prey is in sight, he has stopped barking, his silence rendering him even more ominous. And he is better trained for moments like this than I am.

I have maybe three seconds before he's on me. I abandon any thought of the pepper spray or indeed of freeing my left hand from inside the dry suit. I turn my right side toward him and let him approach. I see my supposition that his handler had let go of him during his fall is true: a sturdy, leather leash is attached to the back of his studded collar. I make this my target. Planting my legs firmly I prepare for battle.

Good luck is something I never factor into a plan. Reliance upon good luck is in the plans of fools; the inevitability of bad luck is in the plans of the wise. However, when good luck occurs, I always take full advantage of it.

Just as the dog comes to within three feet of me, the air is rent with four explosions happening so close together they might almost be one. My pursuers picked themselves up and continued along the trail in hot pursuit, eyes and flashlights trained upon the path beneath their feet. The stomach of the unhappy soul in the lead has pushed up against the black filament tripwire and Stammo's six home-made pipe bombs, placed strategically along the path, have detonated, wreaking havoc upon the leader and anyone else within twenty yards of his rear.

That this happens at all is not luck.

That it happens at the very instant the dog is so close to me, is.

The explosion and the concomitant screams of the wounded, both human and canine, cause the dog to turn his head in the direction of the chaos, allowing me to grab at the leash where it joins his collar. I yank him toward me and manage to slip my fingers under the collar right at the back of his neck, safe from the snapping jaws.

On dry land this dog would be impossible to control; he must weigh one hundred and twenty pounds, he is bigger than he at first looked. However, in the water, he can gain no purchase with his feet and I am able to force him under. His muscular body contorts wildly in an effort to free himself and my disadvantage is that my left hand is still stuck uselessly in the pocket of my pants, trapped under the elastic fabric of the dry suit.

Struggling to maintain both grip and balance, I straighten the fingers of my left hand and, pushing hard against the inside of the suit with my forearm, I am able to slide it from its trap. My relief lasts about a microsecond as the dog executes an amazing wrenching movement at just the moment my hand comes free, causing me to lose my balance and fall forward into the murky water.

Fear lances through me. Thanks to the Bookman, I'm going to die on this island.

4

CAL

TUESDAY, 8 DAYS EARLIER.

"Christ, Rogan! You were there to provide intelligence not to nearly get yourself killed." Nick Stammo is madder than a wasp in a jar. "We were hired to have you check the crowd for familiar faces from your druggie days; not to take 'em down."

I don't have the energy to take exception to his 'druggie days' reference and I don't have the energy to argue with him. "I know, you're right." I'm all for the quiet life.

"Plus you did it for free, for fuck's sake." Nick is not about to be mollified. "This business is hanging by a thread financially and you give away your time for *free*."

In a minute he's going to start on his it's-OK-for-you-with-your-goddamn-trust-fund-but-I-gotta-earn-a-living rant.

"You know I owe Larry Corliss big time," I say. "When he was Mayor he got me back into the Department. He persuaded the Deputy Chief to hire me back and—"

"Yes and you quit a few months later." He shakes his head. "Jeez."

The partnership of Stammo Rogan Investigations Inc. is not unused to these conflicts in spite of which we still make a pretty good team.

"Anyway," he says, "I got us a paying gig."

"Way to go Nick. What is it?"

He smiles. He does that a lot more these days and it's not creepy like it used to be. The storm has passed. We can slide back into our routines which are a lot less stressful than when we were in the VPD.

One thing that works for us is that I bring in some lucrative corporate work via Arnold and Nick brings in a lot of more interesting work from his network of VPD and RCMP members.

He takes an eight-by-ten photo from a folder on his desk and hands it to me. "This kid is the son of a buddy of mine from Toronto."

A boy in his late teens or early twenties, with a small strawberry birthmark on his chin, smiles out of the pic at me. "Missing?" I ask.

"Nah. He's living out here but his folks are worried about him. I got his address."

"So what does his dad want us to do?" I ask.

"Talk to him. Get him to see sense and go home."

"Nick, we're a detective agency, not counselors."

"I know that Rogan…" His voice drops, "but this is important to me."

"Why would he listen to us?"

"I dunno, but I promised his dad. The kid's name's Tyler. Years ago, when they were in grades one and two, Tyler and my son Matt were best buddies. He was a good little kid. I worked with his dad in the OPP. We were all pretty close, went camping together, stuff like that. I want to help him. It'd be like, I dunno, like helping my own kid."

In all the time I've known Stammo, he has only once mentioned his children.

"How are your kids, Nick?"

"I dunno." He sighs. "I haven't had any contact with 'em for must be, what, ten years." He thumps the arm of his wheelchair. "They don't even know I'm in this." He is silent for a while. "It's probably best."

He sighs.

"Anyways, I wanna see if I can turn Tyler around. My buddy's got some money put by and he can afford our rates and with you doing work for free, I think we need to take any paying jobs we can."

I shrug. I can't argue with him, even if he's tilting at windmills with this one.

"What's his address?" I ask.

Stammo flips open the green file folder. There is one document inside.

"According to his dad, he's on the westside, not too far from your place. Ten-thirteen Stephens Street."

I do the math in my head. "That means he lives in English Bay. The northernmost block of Stephens is the fifteen-hundred block, I think. You'd better check the address with your buddy."

An expletive explodes from Stammo's mouth. "I'll check but he was pretty sure of the address."

"Looks like a bigger job than you thought." I can't help being just a bit smug. I have spent a large part of my working life baiting Stammo and I guess I've got into the habit.

"Good. More billing," he grunts.

"What do you want me to do on this one?" I ask.

"Nothing. I owe it to my buddy to do this myself."

It's a change in our dynamic. I usually do the field work and Nick takes care of the office and does the research; jobs at which he is surprisingly very effective.

We settle into our routines. We are doing some investigative work for a law firm trying to track down former employees of a bankrupt airline. It is boring but lucrative work. I am working down a list of names of people who have moved since they worked for the airline, Googling and Facebooking each one to make a connection. Stammo is doing the same thing but in esoteric databases like Lexis-Nexis which he seems to understand.

It's boring and I love it. I have had enough excitement in my forty years to last a lifetime. My life is back together in a good way. I've been clean and sober for just over a year and a half and the thoughts of heroin are abating a little more with time, I get to spend lots of time with my darling Ellie and even my relationship with Sam is...

My cell snaps me out of my wandering thoughts. I don't recognize the caller's name.

"Cal Rogan," I say.

The voice is female, deep and vibrant; the tone is urgent.

She tells me why she is calling and what she wants me to do.

I know I cannot possibly refuse her.

I'm hooked.

5

CAL

WEDNESDAY, 8 DAYS LATER.

Before I hit the water I manage a good lungful of air and, as my head plunges below the surface, I focus all my strength on keeping the dog both at arm's length and under the water. With my left hand, I get a second grip on his collar, then, spreading my legs, I arch my back and, ignoring the pain from my wound, use my stomach muscles to keep him under the water, succeeding in doing this partly because of the weight of the pack on my back.

As his body comes into contact with the bottom, his feet gain a degree of purchase and he renews his struggle, sending billowing clouds of sand through the water, but he and I both know he's beaten. Soon his lungs fill with water and his energy is sapped away. When his feeble wriggles stop, I let go with one hand and push myself to my knees, gulping in the night air as my head breaks the surface.

For safety's sake, I hold the corpse below the water for a further thirty seconds. I feel waves of guilt for killing this dog and the others who were caught in my booby trap. Innocents caught up in the battles of men.

What has become of me? I feel guilt for killing dogs but none for maiming humans.

I try to recover and take inventory of my situation. Our well-laid plans have *gang aft a-gley*: I am wounded; underneath my dry suit, I am soaking; and worse, my exertions with the dog have aggravated the wound. As I recover my breath, I become acutely aware of the increasing pain in my side, previously kept on low by the adrenaline surge of combat. Am I seriously damaged and in need of medical attention?

I release the sad corpse of the dog, which floats lazily to the surface on his left side. I flex the fingers of my right hand as I wade toward the dinghy. I know the uninjured hunters will be proceeding very warily but they will soon be here.

I must work quickly.

First, zip up my dry suit, pull up the hood and pull the face mask down over my eyes and nose. Reach into the bottom of the boat for the control mechanism beside Manny's plastic foot. Press the power switch and then the red arming switch.

Throw in the backpack with all my gear in it. Secure it with the straps installed in the boat. Unhook the boat from its makeshift anchor, maneuver it out of the reeds into the open water and use the electric starter to fire up the motor. It starts on the first try. I switch on the running lights and the orange flashing beacon.

I am about to point the boat out toward open water when I realize, with a rush of fear, that I have forgotten two vital items. From the bottom of the boat, I remove four long, thin plastic tubes, carefully prepared, and slide them into a loop on the thigh of my dry suit, a loop made specifically to hold them. Then I take a weight belt and strap it around my waist.

Done.

I point the boat at the wide mouth of the bay and twist the throttle grip to its fully open position. The dinghy leaps forward eagerly and races out across the water, Manny sitting jauntily at the helm.

Although I can't hear them, I know the noise of the motor will have caused a reaction from my hunters.

Now comes the tricky part.

While still shielded from the woods by the reeds, I hyper-ventilate for fifteen seconds, focusing my attention on the second patch of reeds some seventy yards down the shore. With a final deep breath, I slip beneath the water and, weighed to the bottom by the belt, part swim and part crawl slowly but steadily toward my temporary home.

An Olympic swimmer can swim seventy meters in around thirty seconds. I'm twice the age with less than half the skill and have to cover the distance under water with a bullet wound in my side which is aggravated by the movements of the breaststroke. Thirty seconds: I start to let little breaths of air out of my lungs, silently praying no guards are yet out of the woods and if they are, that their focus is on the retreating boat.

Forty-five seconds: my lungs start to hurt. Sixty seconds: the pain starts to rival the pain in my side and stars appear before my eyes. I must go up for air.

I pray I won't be seen.

The surface is three feet above my head. Exhale the last dribbles of air. Push up from the bottom. Break the surface. Greedily fill my lungs. Dive back down.

I struggle on, dreading that I was seen.

As my lungs start to burst for a second time, I see through the water, illuminated by the Maglite, that I've reached the second patch of reeds. I pull my knees underneath me and carefully push my head above the water to gasp in air as silently as I can. I have reached the outer edge to the second patch of reeds. I snap off the light.

Trusting that no one will notice the black-clad head just slightly above the water, I turn in the direction of the forest. Where the path makes its exit, a guard steps out from the trees. He turns back and calls to someone then faces back out toward the ocean. Kalashnikov to his shoulder, he aims toward the escaping dinghy and fires off a dozen rounds to no effect. He slings the weapon back over his shoulder, takes a walkie-talkie from his belt and barks some orders into it, almost certainly alerting the crew of the yellow cigarette-boat on the other side of the island. I smile. At least this part of the plan seems on track.

Discretion being the better part of valor, I take a deep breath and slide below the surface. I swim around the outer edge of the reeds for about ten yards and then, proceeding carefully, worm my way into the middle of the reed patch, trying desperately to avoid causing the slender stalks to wave.

Now to make my bed and lie on it.

I remove two of the specially prepared tubes from the loop on my thigh and blow the water out of them as I raise them above the surface. I breathe through them, rest my head on the sandy bottom, loosen the weight belt and pull it up over my chest.

I am invisible.

My body is four feet below the water, obscured from anyone not standing directly above. The only sign: the two tubes rising above the surface, indistinguishable from the thousands of reeds surrounding them. Even someone with infrared field glasses will be unable to isolate the minimal difference in temperature between the night air and my exhalations among the reeds. I settle down for the night.

I take stock. I am warm but as the reaction to my exertions wears off, will the chill of the water become a problem? Mercifully, despite the punishment it has taken, the wound in my side is just a dull ache; I hope it lasts. I risk using the Maglite to illuminate my watch: eight fifteen. I wonder if the decoy will work.

Some sounds come to me through the water but they are indistinct, of unknown nature and source.

As I begin to relax, I feel a pressure in my bowel and my bladder, a common reaction to an intense period of stress. I want to suppress my human sensibilities and let go but I dare not. The risk of infecting my wound is too great. Out of spite, my side starts to throb. It's going to be an uncomfortable night.

The water mutes the boom. Atta boy Stammo.

Two panels—cut out of the hull and then replaced using the least possible amount of epoxy glue and just enough plastique—blow out and the dinghy, together with Manny and my equipment, take the one hundred and fifty meter trip to the bottom of the Strait of Georgia, leaving nothing for the cigarette-boat to examine and burying all evidence of my visit to the island.

I am alone with my thoughts.

Now I have time to wallow in my guilt.

The full impact of what I have done assails me with the words of King Richard, so faultlessly crafted: *O, no! alas, I rather hate myself, For hateful deeds committed by myself!*

I have crossed the line.

The big line.

No matter how I try and justify it, I have done the unthinkable.

Three times. And the third is the worst.

And it all started just eight long days ago at one outrageously expensive lunch where Rebecca Bradbury asked for our help. The solution seemed so logical when we planned it. Hell, it *was* logical. We just didn't plan for one element.

Despite my one year, six months and eighteen days of sobriety, I can't help thinking how just one little hit of heroin would blunt both my pain and my disgust.

6

CAL

TUESDAY, 8 DAYS EARLIER.

T he Yew Restaurant in the Four Seasons is a bit out of my price range. Correction. It's a lot out of my price range but this is where she asked to meet. I scan the menu while I am waiting for Rebecca Bradbury, trying to plan the lowest-cost meal; a salad is usually a good choice. The lobster sandwich looks great but at forty-five bucks, I'll pass. If I stick with the parsnip soup and the Caesar salad, my side of the bill will come out to less than thirty bucks; I just hope that Mrs. Bradbury doesn't have much of an appetite. In her position, I wouldn't.

I am wearing my only suit. I'm glad I made the choice. The place is riddled with suits, most of them costing more than the net worth of Stammo Rogan Investigations Inc. I feel out of place. Not so long ago I was a homeless junkie, living on the streets of the downtown east side. I could have lived for a month on what this lunch is going to cost.

"Mister Rogan?"

I stand and extend my hand. Rebecca Bradbury is very tall, almost as tall as me. She is dressed in a cream-colored suit with a maroon purse and shoes. Her ash-blonde hair is perfectly coiffed and styled to show off her earrings. A necklace of large pearls circles her long neck. Everything from her smile to her shoes screams old money. She is stunning.

She looks to be in her mid-thirties but behind the façade, and the artfully applied makeup, is the face of a woman who has not slept for a while and who is racked with worry.

"So nice of you to see me at such short notice."

An elegant movement of her hand invites me to take my seat. The maître d' who escorted her to the table, pulls out her chair.

"Would you bring me a glass of Pol Roger?" she asks him. Twenty-nine bucks if my memory of the wine list serves me.

"Of course, Mrs. Bradbury." He looks at me and raises an eyebrow. "For you sir?"

"Just water, I'm driving." I'm not. Our office is five blocks away.

"San Pellegrino?"

I wonder what that's going to cost in this place. Hopefully less than a glass of wine. What the heck, I'll splurge. "That would be fine."

I do not want to make small talk; we'll have little in common. "How can I help you in the matter of your daughter's disappearance?" I ask.

She appears a little taken aback by the direct approach. "Well," she gathers her thoughts for a second. "While I have full confidence in the Vancouver Police Department, Ariel's disappearance is one of many cases for them, so Ariel's father and I thought it would be good to get some additional help. David, that's Mr. Bradbury, asked the advice of Arnold Young; Mr. Young's firm worked with my late father's firm. He gave us your phone number and a glowing recommendation. He said you'd solved the murder of Kevin Wallace; we knew Mr. Wallace of course and still see Mrs. Wallace socially from time to time. Mr. Young said we could trust you completely."

From Arnold, that's high praise indeed.

"Of course," I say, "I checked on the newspaper reports of Ariel's disappearance and will do anything I can to help. I have a daughter, Ellie; she's the same age. She was once taken by someone," I shudder inside at the memory, "so I have an idea of what you must be experiencing right now."

She nods, smiles and looks very vulnerable.

"Tell me what happened," I suggest gently.

"She didn't come home from school on Friday. She goes to St. Cecelia's."

It's the same school Ellie goes to, courtesy of my trust fund from Mr. Wallace. Something tells me not to volunteer this information.

"She didn't attend the last class of the day after afternoon recess. During recess, she was talking to one of her friends and then she went to the washroom. No one saw her again. No one saw her leave the school, she just disappeared into thin air." There is a quiver in her voice. She is working hard to keep it all together.

"Have you and your husband received any ransom demands?"

She looks uncomfortable. I get the impression she is holding something back… or is about to.

"Mrs. Bradbury…?"

She looks into my eyes, without blinking. It is disconcerting. Then her shoulders sag. "David and I have just recently separated. We are hardly talking, even about this. For my part I have not received any ransom demands. You would need to talk to David and ask him the same question." She searches through her purse and retrieves a business card which she hands to me. *Sotto voce*, she adds, "No one in our circle knows about the separation. I trust in your complete discretion on the subject."

I nod. "Did you tell the police about your separation?" I ask.

She shakes her head.

Clearly, I do not understand the very rich. Why would you keep such a material fact from the police investigating your daughter's disappearance?

"Did Ariel know?"

"Yes. I told her on Wednesday evening." She looks devastated; she is wondering where on earth her daughter can be.

"Do you think your separation might have anything to do with her disappearance?" As I say the words, I catch the tone in my voice.

So does she.

Before she can reply the waiter arrives and asks us if we are ready to order.

She has not looked at the menu but orders the bisque followed by the lobster sandwich. I toy with the idea of dropping the soup and saving twelve bucks but it's not going to make that much difference.

When the waiter has left, she answers my question. "If you are suggesting that David might have taken her to get at me, I very much doubt it. Frankly, he doesn't have the stones."

The crudity sounds strange delivered in her patrician tones.

"Actually, I was wondering if perhaps Ariel was upset by the separation and might have run away in order to punish you both."

She takes this like a slap and for the first time I see the complete devastation on her face. My heart goes out to her and I regret the tone of my voice. I am going to bring her daughter back. No matter what. *And* I'm going to do it before the VPD.

"Ariel would never..." she starts to say. Then she thinks. "If she did, where would she go?"

"Typically a kid will go to a friend's house."

"The police talked to her friends and their parents. They are sure that didn't happen."

"Do you have a recent photo of her?"

She goes to her purse and takes out a five-by-seven picture.

It is a head-and-shoulders portrait. Ariel is sitting on a high-backed chair, wearing a sequined dress. She is a very pretty girl and she looks a lot like her mother but... there's something wrong.

"Did she have a boyfriend?" I ask.

"Of course not. She's eight years old. Would you allow your daughter to have a boyfriend at that age?"

Without showing my surprise that she is only eight, I reply, "No, of course not. But we don't always have control over what our children choose to do when they're not with us."

"Not Ariel; she was very focused."

"On what?" I ask.

She is silent as the waiter places the first course in front of us.

As soon as he is out of earshot, she continues. "On her schoolwork, on her sports. She was very good at field hockey. She had all sorts of outside interests: horseback riding, gymnastics, but mostly singing and dancing. She really didn't have the time or, for that matter, the opportunity to have a boyfriend."

As we eat, she talks about Ariel's dancing, singing and sports prowess but I am only half listening. There is something about the photograph that feels wrong. Ariel just doesn't look like your average eight-year-old girl. But I can't quite put my finger on why.

A busboy clears the plates and the waiter brings the main course. Rebecca orders another glass of champagne. The bill for this lunch is heading toward two hundred dollars; Stammo is going to have a cow.

I ask all the usual questions about Ariel's routines, her friends and everything that happened during the days leading up to her disappearance. Rebecca's answers are mostly very clear except when it comes to Ariel's friends. She writes down their names and suggests I talk to them.

When I have run out of questions, we come to the part of the conversation I really don't like: the part where we talk about fees. This is usually done by Stammo, who seems to have no difficulty with it. I take a folded sheet of paper from my inside breast pocket and hand it to her. "This is our schedule of fees and expenses which you may—"

"I am sure they're just fine," she says; she takes the paper from me and without unfolding it puts it in her purse. She removes a check from her checkbook. "I presume a retainer of ten thousand will be sufficient."

I do a great job in covering my amazement. "Yes. That would be fine. Thank you," I say.

She hands me the check and I manage to avoid looking at it before sliding it into my pocket.

With no further ado she stands, her lobster sandwich hardly touched. "I want a daily report every evening from you on your progress, starting this evening. Thank you. I am putting a great deal of faith in you."

She turns and makes her exit.

As she goes out, I realize I didn't get to learn a lot about Ariel. But I do know one person who can give me some unbiased information.

As I look toward the exit, the words 'dine and dash' slip through my mind.

I wonder where Ariel is. I suspect either she has run away, though eight year-olds don't usually get that far, or her father has taken her. But if I'm wrong, wherever she is, she will likely be terrified. I imagine Ellie out there held against her will. People who abduct children are scum. I'm glad that we've got this assignment. I swear I'm going to find her and return her to her mother, no matter what. This case is already under my skin and best of all, there is no connection with the world of drugs, the world I never want to visit again.

The waiter comes over and, with a little less trepidation than I had before taking the ten-grand retainer, I ask for the bill.

"It's covered, sir," he says. "We have Mrs. Bradbury's card on file. She comes here for lunch or dinner several times a week."

Stammo will be pleased on all counts.

7

CAL

I have never worked in an office. As a cop I avoided the office as much as I could. I wanted to be out on the streets whenever possible. However, over the last year or so, I have visited some very plush offices. But this office beats the heck out of all of them.

The discreet brass plate outside, polished to perfection, announces to the world that these are the offices of Bentley and Bradbury, Merchant Bancorp, whatever that means.

I am sitting in the reception area drinking coffee from fine Wedgwood china, served by a receptionist who looks like she should be on TV, advertising shampoo. So many cases of missing children involve the other parent that I may be able to wrap this up today using some tactics the police can't use. It would be nice to have a simple, no-stress resolution. When a secretary comes to fetch me, it is with some anticipation that I get up off the soft leather sofa.

As I follow her down the hallway, I note that the paintings are all original oils or acrylics. They are all equally stunning. One looks like a Jackson Pollock; could it possibly be an original?

David Bradbury is standing in the doorway of his office.

His face is familiar but I can't place it. He shakes my hand and draws me inside. "Thank you so much for coming Mr. Rogan," he says. He is warm and friendly and I take an instant liking to him, though it doesn't offset the pang I feel at being Mr. Rogan rather than Detective Rogan. I ask myself, not for the first time, whether I did the right thing when I quit the VPD to go into business with Stammo.

"If there's anything you can do to help find Ariel…" he leaves the sentence hanging and a wave of empathy sweeps through me. If Ellie were missing like this, I would be beside myself with worry. "The police call me every day and update me but nothing seems to be happening. There are no leads, nothing shows on the school CCTV cameras, no one saw her leave the school premises. *Nothing.* Anything you can do… anything." The desperation in his voice is palpable. Unless he's the world's best actor, I can write off the spousal kidnapping theory. Damn, I was hoping for a quick and quiet conclusion to the case.

He is the opposite of his soon-to-be-former wife. She was controlled, only letting the grief slip through for instants here and there; he is a mess.

He leads me to a meeting area and we sit.

"There are three possibilities," I say. "Firstly that Ariel has simply run away. She may be upset at the breakup between you and your wife." His face registers surprise that I know this. "Or she may have run away for some other reason. Secondly she may have been kidnapped for ransom…" In the pause, I scrutinize his face for any reaction to this suggestion. "You are obviously a wealthy man Mr. Bradbury. Have you received any ransom demands?"

He doesn't answer immediately. He looks at me, undecided. There is an internal struggle going on, I can read it in his face. Then he comes to some conclusion. "No. No ransom demand yet."

I think I believe him but he is covering up something. Not good.

"Is there anything else you want to tell me?" I ask him fixing him with a steady gaze.

"No. Nothing." His expression is blank. It looks forced.

"If you were to receive a ransom demand, would you pay it?"

"Yes, of course." Again, I sense something is wrong with his answer.

"If you received a ransom demand, would you tell the police about it?"

He ruminates.

Ten long seconds pass. "No."

"Would you tell me?"

"I might."

"You should," I say.

He shrugs.

"We also have to consider a third possibility," I say.

He puts his head in his hands. He knows what's coming.

"Ariel may have been kidnapped but not for money."

He lifts his head to look at me and tears are rolling down his face. "I can't even think about that," he says. I double my pledge to find Ariel and find her fast.

He may have to think the unthinkable. Ariel has been missing for four full days now and, unless either he or Rebecca is lying, there has been no ransom demand. It's a big 'unless'. I can't shake the feeling that David Bradbury is hiding something.

"What do you do here Mr. Bradbury?"

"I'm the CEO, I run the company."

"I assume Mr. Bentley is your partner?"

He gives the hint of a smile. "No, Mr. Bentley doesn't exist." He sees my puzzlement. "I am the sole owner of the company but it's a marketing thing. The company name seems more substantial if it implies there are partners. I chose the name Bentley because it sounds solid and respectable, like a Bentley car."

It sounds a bit shady to my unbusiness-like ears. Go figure.

I'm still uneasy about what he might not have told me. "What does your company do?"

"We are a type of merchant bank. People with high net worth place their money with us and we invest it in a variety of companies, giving them much higher returns than they could make in say a mutual fund."

Out of my league for sure.

"How many people have placed their money with you?"

That same look of discomfort crosses his face. "I uh... can't discuss specifics. Confidentiality agreements, you know?"

I press harder. "Well is it hundreds of people?"

"Oh. No. We have a small number of clients but with exceptional net worth."

"Have you ever lost money for your clients?"

"Never." He says it emphatically but I know he's lying this time; it's written on his face.

I continue as though he had said yes. "Could one of them be so angry that he wanted to get to you somehow?"

"No, no. That's preposterous." But his face tells me that maybe he has a suspicion.

"If there was, who would it be?" I press him.

"As I said before, I cannot divulge client names to you." So there is someone; otherwise a plain 'No one' or 'I don't know' would have sufficed.

I'm not going to get anything more going down that rabbit hole, so I change tack. "Your wife told me that Arnold Young had recommended me to you," he nods as I continue. "Is he a client?"

"Good heavens no. I know him through Mr. Wallace. I wondered if his security firm could help."

His answer surprises me. The *good heavens no* implies that either Arnold doesn't have the money to be considered a 'high-net-worth' client or that Arnold would never consider investing. Seeing as Arnold manages the late Mr. Wallace's money he would certainly qualify as high net worth. Note to self: check him out with Arnold.

Although there is something amiss here, it may be nothing to do with Ariel's disappearance. High finance may be a business segment riddled with white-collar crime; it is not usually a reason for abduction. I am getting a creeping and horrible suspicion that the motive for her kidnapping is not financial. I can feel a real anger building towards whoever took her. I redouble the pledge.

I can feel the thrill of the hunt: the thing that drove me as a cop. My hope that this was a parental kidnapping disappears and I realize that I didn't really want that anyway.

I have to face the naked truth: I need this.

8

STAMMO

Tyler's Dad said he couldn't think of any reason why his son would have come out to BC but I've got a good idea. After a call to an old buddy in North America's oldest municipal police force, I've got a *real* good idea. Tyler's dad, Bob, is an old-style cop like me. He failed to tell me his son got busted a couple of times by the Toronto Police Service for possession of pot. It's tough for a cop to admit his kid's broken the law. When Matt got arrested the first time, I was goddamn embarrassed by it. Anyway, if the cops in Toronto are anything like the cops in Vancouver they pretty much ignore possession. I'm thinking Tyler may have had larger amounts, warranting possession with intent to distribute, but they went easy on him because of his old man.

For a kid into dealing, Vancouver's a great place to be: lots of dope, lots of users and cops who ain't interested in small-time action. At Hastings and Main—known by many as Wastings and Pain—people used to do deals on the street within half a block of the old Main Street Police Station.

Tyler's pretty much invisible on social media. His Facebook page hasn't been updated for over a year and there's no sign of him on Twitter or Instagram. I'm betting he's out there somewhere but under a new identity.

There's nothing in the court records here either.

I've tried a couple of times to hack into the VPD system but it's beyond my skill level so I have to rely on my buddies there to look things up for me. I don't like asking but this kid is like a second son to me; he's worth cashing in some of my markers.

Maybe I'll ask Bob to do the same for me. See if he can find out where Matt is at.

I'd give anything to see him and Lucy again.

9

CAL

C limbing these stairs always makes me feel sad. Sad for what I almost regained and then lost. But for Ellie, I don't like coming here anymore; it just churns up the past.

"Oh, hello Detective Rogan." Cora Hunt, Sam's neighbor, is coming down the stairs, reusable shopping bags in hand.

"Hello Mrs. Hunt." I don't correct her use of the title; I don't have time to get into the necessary explanations.

As I reach the top of the stairs, I hear, "Hi Daddy." Ellie is standing in the doorway, beaming; she must have seen me through the front window.

"Hi Sweetie." She runs into my arms and I lift her and spin her around in a great big hug. Although she is eight and a half she still doesn't weigh much.

Sam appears from the kitchen and I feel the accustomed tug in my chest. "Come in Cal. Oh—" she catches herself, "I mean, come in Rocky."

"It's OK, Sam. You know what? I'd rather you called me Cal."

A couple of years ago, I decided that I would like to be called Rocky, a tribute to Roy. But now, in my mind, Rocky is the drug addict part of me, the part that will always hear the Beast inside with its siren call, willing me to take just one more hit of heroin. Cal was my name before all that.

Sam smiles. "Good." She leans in as though about to kiss me on the cheek then thinks better of it. Ellie, who misses nothing, pulls me down to her level and plants a kiss on my cheek instead.

"Thanks for letting me come to see Ellie," I say. "I needed to talk to her and couldn't wait until the weekend."

"No prob," she smiles. The room lights up for me. It is the smile I fell in love with fourteen years ago. "Listen. Ellie and I were just about to have dinner. It's beef stroganoff. Why don't you eat with us? There's lots."

I stamp on the conflicting emotions and say, "I'd love to."

"You go in the living room and have your chat with Ellie. I'll call you when it's ready."

Sam's apartment is in an old Shaughnessy mansion, converted into a fourplex. The developer did a wonderful job of keeping the old feel of the building while completely renovating the interior. I walk Ellie over to the large bay window and we sit on the built-in bench.

I look at my wonderful daughter and my heart feels like it wants to burst. "Ell, I want you to help me with something but it is very important that you don't speak to anyone about what we discuss, especially not the people at school, OK?"

"Can I speak to Mommy about it?" she asks.

"Of course. But nobody else."

She nods. "OK, Daddy."

"It's about someone at your school, Ariel Bradbury. Do you know her?"

"Yes." The single syllable is drawn out over a second.

"Do you like her?"

"She's OK. She's in my music class."

"But she's not one of your friends?"

"Not really. She only hangs out with the cool girls, like

Megan and Kaylee." A worried look comes on to her face. "Ashleigh told me that the police went to Megan's house on the weekend and to Kaylee's. They said that she was missing and they asked a lot of questions."

"Is Ashleigh a friend of Ariel too?"

"Yes. But Ash is nice, don't you remember, you met her at my birthday party? She's probably Ariel's best friend but Ariel's Mom doesn't like her." I don't remember Ashleigh but I can imagine that Rebecca Bradbury would be very controlling about her daughter's friends. Also I don't remember the name on the list of Ariel's friends given to me by Rebecca.

"Do you know why Mrs. Bradbury doesn't like Ashleigh?"

"Oh yes. It's because of that beauty thing... you know... on TV."

She laughs at the look of mystification on my face. "You know Daddy. That show on TV where all these girls compete to be like beauty queens. *Canada's Littlest Beauty*."

"Ashleigh was on the show?" I could see Rebecca Bradbury not approving of someone on a reality TV show.

"No, silly. Ariel was on the show."

"Ariel was on a reality TV show?" Why in heaven's name did Rebecca Bradbury not mention this to me?

"Yes. It's on tonight."

This I have to see. I get back on track with, "But why is it that Mrs. Bradbury doesn't like Ashleigh?"

"It's because last week Ariel told Ash that she didn't want to be on the show anymore and Ash told her she had to tell her mom and say she wouldn't do it anymore. When Ariel told her mom, she freaked. She told Ariel she couldn't speak to Ash ever again. She even came to the school and complained to the principal."

An uneasy feeling worms its way into my gut.

"Do you know why Ariel wanted to stop being on the show?"

"No. Ash didn't say."

"When the police talked to Ariel's other friends, did they talk to Ashleigh too?"

"No."

"Three minutes," Sam's voice calls out from the kitchen.

Ellie leaps to her feet. "Yummeeeee. I'm starving." She makes a beeline for the kitchen.

"Wash hands first," I remind her. She veers off toward the powder room and I follow.

As we lather our hands, I ask, "Ell, I want you to think carefully about this. Did you notice anything unusual at school on Friday?"

She thinks. "We had fish cakes for lunch. They were gross."

"Anything else?"

"Is that when Ariel went missing?" she asks.

"Yes."

"Maybe the policewoman saw something."

"What policewoman?"

"She was in the playground during afternoon recess. She talked to some of us."

"Is she often at your school?" The VPD has a program that assigns patrol officers to schools but they usually go to schools with high at-risk populations, not westside private schools. It's a sign of the times, I guess.

"I've never seen her before. She was nice and very pretty. She had hair like Mommy's. I told her you used to be a policeman and asked her if she knew you, but she didn't. I told her I wanted to be a policewoman too."

"Do you remember if she talked to Ariel?"

"No."

Hands clean and dried, we head for the delicious smells wafting from the kitchen.

———

I CAN'T BELIEVE what I'm seeing. I glance at Sam and she seems unmoved. Ellie is glued to the TV.

Canada's Littlest Beauty is a reality show where a bunch of little girls compete to win a cross between a beauty pageant and a talent show. What appalls me is that they are all wearing makeup, are dressed inappropriately and are dancing and parading about in an overtly sexual way. Is this fundamentally wrong or am I just getting old? Am I turning into my straightlaced mother?

The mothers on the show are definitely not straightlaced.

They all seem to be pressuring their daughters excessively and by far the worst is Rebecca Bradbury. My client stands out in another way too: all the other mothers on the show seem to be overweight and under-intelligent.

As I look at the show I become more and more appalled at the ways in which Ariel is being forced to perform. Apparently, all the contestants are competing to be in a beauty pageant that is going to take place in Toronto. Ariel is seen being coached by singing, dancing and gymnastics teachers and I make a mental note to look into the backgrounds of her tutors. All the mothers are very demanding of their kids but Rebecca goes beyond the pale. At one point she screams at Ariel for messing up a dance number.

In this episode, the girls are competing in a local talent show in the Fraser Valley. In the run up to the contest, we see Rebecca doing little things to undermine the other contestants: a comment here, a derisive laugh there, all nasty little tactics.

When the contest begins, I feel myself becoming increasingly angry. The girls are dressed in swimsuits, some with tiny skirts; they all are wearing hair extensions in adult styles and are heavily made up. Many of the girls have devices like a boxer's mouth guard which gives them the look of having perfect, very white, very adult-looking teeth.

Then it hits me.

Ariel's photo. I know why it looked wrong to me. She was wearing a sequined dress, probably bought for this show. She was very subtly made up to look like an adult.

The children parade around the stage in what seems to me to be sexually provocative ways and I can't suppress the mental image of pedophiles everywhere glued to their TVs, touching themselves in ecstasy.

As soon as the show ends, Ellie gets up from her place between us on the couch and goes upstairs to have her bath and get ready for bed.

Sam is lounging in old sweats and a T-shirt yet looks stunningly elegant in that way only Sam can pull off. I feel a catch in my throat as I look at her and curse myself again for what I have thrown away.

"What did you think about that show?" I ask her.

"In fairly poor taste, I'd say."

"Poor taste! It's bordering on pedophilia." My voice has crept up a decibel or two.

"I think that's a bit of an overreaction." I can't believe she is not as outraged as I am.

"An overreaction. You have *got* to be kidding." That was more of a shout. "It's—"

"Cal, please." Her voice is distressed. "I don't want to argue with you. This was a lovely evening. Please, don't spoil it."

There is a sadness in her eyes which deflates my anger.

"What's the matter, Sam?"

"Nothing." A sure sign there is.

Direct questioning won't work; I just stay silent, looking at her.

"Why did you quit the Department?" she asks.

Not the question I was expecting.

"Long story," I say.

"We have all night."

I look at her and wonder what she may mean by that but her face gives nothing away.

"Well you know what happened with my colleagues?" I say. She nods. "Well... I guess that it just kind of broke the bond of trust you need when you're a cop. So I started to think about my life with the VPD and realized that twice in the last couple of years, Ellie was put in a lot of danger and that you could easily have been killed, both as a direct result of cases I was working on. So—"

"Both those were as much my fault as yours," she says. It's the first time Sam has made any reference to these incidents, let alone ascribed any self-blame.

"Either way," I continue, "I didn't want to have either of you in danger because of what I do for a living. I was also feeling very guilty about my failure to contain the situation that put Stammo in that wheelchair—we both know he's there because of me—so when he suggested starting the firm..." I shrug.

She smiles and takes a long breath. "Cal, I need to ask you something."

"Ask away." My feelings belie my casual tone.

"It's been just over a year since..." My heart drops, I know what's coming. "Well... since we stood in the kitchen, in this house, and said that we still loved each other."

I am silenced by my feelings of guilt but Sam takes my silence for something else. "You do remember that Cal?" There is an edge of sarcasm in her voice.

"Yes." I fail to keep the frustration out of mine.

"I know you were consumed by the case you were on, the murder of that poor boy, but when it was all over... nothing. It was like what we had said never happened."

"I know, Sam. I'm sorry."

"But why Cal?" A tear is starting to form in the corner of her eye.

My guilt is weighing me down. I can't tell her the truth.

No matter what the extenuating circumstances, if I told her it would hurt her so much that... Or am I fooling myself? Am I just too ashamed to admit it?

The silence is palpable. I have to say something. Why can't I just tell her the truth, tell her I love her, take her in my arms and smother her in kisses?

One look at her face decides it for me. The tear that was forming in her eye is running down the side of her nose, being chased by another. I have to man up to the truth, ask forgiveness and let the cards lie where they fall. My hero knew this: *For they breathe truth that breathe their words in pain.*

"Sam—"

"Ta-daaahh." Ellie leaps into the room. Hair wet and face still glowing from the bath; she is wearing some of Sam's makeup, not at all inexpertly applied, and is sporting a swimming costume and a pair of Sam's high-heeled shoes.

In a parody of *Canada's Littlest Beauty,* she cavorts across the living room gyrating in what she fondly imagines to be a sexy dance number.

I am confounded by a mélange of emotions: frustration at losing my moment with Sam; amusement at Ellie's hilarious antics; horror at the explicitness of her dance routine and, overall, sadness at the passing of innocence.

But, as it so often does, humor comes to the rescue. Sam starts chuckling and the floodgates open. In moments, we are both caught up in paroxysms of laughter which make Ellie intensify her shenanigans, which in turn, ramp up our mirth, now bordering on hysteria.

I long to feel the touch of Sam's hand and I move to reach across the couch and take it but before my hand has moved three inches, Ellie launches herself into the air and lands, on her knees, between us. Her arms are spread wide to accept the accolades of the crowd which Sam and I dutifully supply.

Sam takes Ellie's hand and stands. "OK young lady, it's time for bed. Let's get that makeup off you. Kiss Daddy good-night." I get a big hug and a kiss on the cheek which I reciprocate.

The laughter has broken the ice. With Ellie in bed, I will be able to tell Sam how I really feel, tell her how much I love her.

Sam gives me that smile I love.

"I'm really glad you came to dinner, Cal. It was lovely to see you. Remember Ellie has a Pro-D day on Friday, you said you'd take her for the afternoon and evening. I'll see you then when you pick her up."

I've been dismissed. I feel a real physical pain and, for the first time in a while, I feel the Beast inside telling me I can wash the pain away with just a small hit of heroin. Just this once.

10

CAL

WEDNESDAY

This place pushes a bunch of my buttons. During my brief return to the VPD I was based here. A lot of the people here know my history and most of them don't like what they know. Stammo usually comes here alone when we are working cases that involve the VPD, but today I came with him. I'm in MCU and he's downstairs talking to a buddy from the drug squad. He thinks Tyler might have shown up on their radar.

Ariel's kidnapping is firmly in the hands of Major Crime and is being worked by Steve Waters, formerly a close colleague, but too much water has gone under the bridge for us to even pretend still to be friends. The only thing we have left is a mutual respect for each other's abilities. It's enough.

He's briefed me on the case but, unfortunately, he has nothing useful that I don't already know. Part of me is appalled at how little their investigation has progressed; maybe it's squeezed budgets or maybe he's not telling me everything. Either way it reinforces my pledge to find her.

"Coming up to five days and no ransom demand…" Steve sighs. "I've got to believe the worst."

"Are you sure the father hasn't had a call?" Steve's ears

prick up at that. "When I went to see him I asked him about it and although he said he hadn't, there was something in his reaction that didn't ring true."

"So you think he's going to go it alone?"

"Maybe. When I asked him whether he'd call you guys if he got a ransom demand he said no."

"Son of a…" Steve's face clouds over. Parents' clandestine attempts to buy back their children are the bane of the cops trying to solve their cases.

"Good news is, if he does get any demands, maybe he's going to call me and, believe me Steve, if he does, I'm going to call you."

"Thanks, Cal. Man, I hope it is kidnapping for money but y'know what? I'm betting this is going to become a murder investigation." He sighs. "You got anything else?"

"Apparently you missed one of her friends in your interviews. I'm going to talk to her after I leave here."

"What's her name?" he asks.

"Ashleigh Jakes."

Steve taps some keys on his keyboard. "Hmmm. You're right, we missed her." He doesn't seem too concerned. "Let me know if she's got anything new."

Before I came here, I decided not to tell Steve about Ariel being on *Canada's Littlest Beauty*. I want to check that out myself first. Maybe it's petty but I want to show him that I'm the better cop. Then again, maybe he already knows.

I get up. "Thanks for giving me the update, Steve. I'll talk to you soon."

"Yeah, Cal. See you."

I head for the door, glad to know I'll soon be out of this building.

"Oh, hey, Cal. I almost forgot. We're charging Guy Chang with attempted murder, parole violation and a bunch of weapons charges. The Crown Prosecution office is going to call you. They want you to give evidence at the trial."

A big smile cracks my face. I will be happy to send Goliath to prison for a second, much longer term. "Sure, Steve. No problem."

I turn to go a second time and then I remember something. Maybe Steve does know more than he's telling me. I'll ask. "Hey Steve, I almost forgot. Did the patrol officer at St. Cecelia's have anything useful?"

"What patrol officer?"

"Apparently there's one assigned there."

"At St. Cecelia's? Are you sure?"

I can feel an icy finger on my spine. "Yes. Ellie talked to her."

He picks up the phone and dials. As he takes in the answer to his question, his face says it all.

The icy finger becomes a knife.

11

ARIEL

I'm worried about Mommy and Daddy. The police lady said they were in a car crash but she won't let me go and see them in the hospital. This house is nice and everything but I've been here for days and days and now I can't stop crying. I miss them so much.

I don't think I'm ever going to see them again.

She told me I've got to be brave but she's left me alone.

Anyway, I'm glad she's gone. I liked her at first but when we got here and she took off her police uniform she wasn't so nice and she took all my stuff. I can't even text Justin.

The garden is huge, even huger than Grandpa's. I can see it through the window and she said if I'm good I'll be allowed out there. I saw the helicopter land a little while ago, just before she left. Maybe it's going to take me back to see Mommy and Daddy.

I hope so. I hope so. I hope so.

I'm starting to feel hungry again. I wonder when the nice old lady will be here with lunch. The food here is really good. Not like that diet stuff Mommy always makes me eat. The lady who brings it doesn't speak English but she's very nice to me, except she makes me wear a big huge bib, like a baby. It's to protect my costumes I suppose.

The police lady must be a bit stupid. The clothes she got for me are all just like costumes from the show, not regular clothes. I'm wearing my favorite one right now, the red sequined swimsuit with the white tights. I love costumes but I don't want to wear them all the time.

There's the sound of the key in the door. Goody. Lunchtime.

It's not the nice lady.

It's a man. He's tall like Daddy. I've seen him before. Oh yes, I remember him. He's nice. And there's another man with him but *he* doesn't look nice.

The nice one takes two steps into the room, looks at me and smiles. "Hello Ariel. Don't you look pretty?" he says.

"Are you going to take me to the hospital to see Mommy and Daddy?" Please, please, please say yes.

"Twirl around," he says. Why didn't he answer my question?

"Are you—" Something in his face makes me stop asking.

He smiles and makes a twirling motion with his finger. I don't like the way he's looking at me. He's smiling but it scares me. I thought he was nice.

I twirl around.

He takes two more steps into the room. I can smell him. It's like the aftershave Daddy wears. "Do it again... Like on the show," he says.

I don't have my ballet shoes and it's carpet anyway but I do as good a pirouette as I can.

"Good," he says. "Now do a curtsey."

I cross my left foot over my right and bob down.

"Hold it right there," he says and I freeze in position.

I don't like where he's looking at me. He takes a step closer. He reaches out and his fingers are trembling.

It's just a gentle pat on the shoulder but then he leaves his hand there. I want to squirm away but I'm afraid it will make him angry.

"Very good," he smiles and squeezes.

He lets go of my shoulder and his hand moves toward my face.

"Not yet," the bad-looking one says. His voice is funny. I don't like it. "When you have done your part of the bargain," he says.

The one I used to think was nice steps back. I can hear his breathing.

Then he turns and leaves. "Very good," I hear as the door clicks shut behind them.

I don't stop crying until I hear the helicopter taking him away.

I want Mommy and Daddy so much.

12

CAL

The patrol guys got here before me. In fact they gave me a hard time and wouldn't let me in until Steve arrived and gave them the OK.

Steve has got a whole team at the school questioning them about the phony policewoman who talked to some of the girls on the Friday Ariel went missing.

Steve and I are about to interview Ashleigh, the girl Ellie says is Ariel's friend but who was not interviewed by the police. Steve didn't really want me involved but I sold him on my being there due to the fact that Ashleigh is Ellie's friend and I have already met her so it may make it easier for her to open up to me. I omitted telling Steve I don't actually remember meeting her. I've got a good feeling that I'm going to get something good from this interview.

We are in one of the school's music rooms. Sitting with us is one of Ashleigh's teachers who is also a school counselor; she is an older woman with a saccharine smile and an eagle eye.

Ashleigh is not the typical St. Cecelia's kid. Despite the school uniform, she has an edgy look to her. Her hair is cut in an uneven punk style and she has the look of an eight- year-old rebel. My recollection of her is vague.

As pre-agreed with Steve, I lead the questioning.

"So Ashleigh, as you know I'm Ellie's dad and I'm helping the police find Ariel. Would it be OK if we asked you a few questions?"

"I guess." No smile but not actively hostile.

"There was a woman here last Friday, dressed as a police officer. Did you speak to her?"

"She wasn't really a policewoman?" She's a sharp kid but there is a note of fear in her voice. The counselor reaches out and strokes her shoulder. I hope that she doesn't get involved in the interview.

"No, she wasn't. Did she say anything to you?"

"Kinda. A few of us were standing around and she came and talked to us."

"What about?" Steve asks.

She glances at him but turns back and speaks to me. "Just about whether we liked the school and what we did for fun, who our friends were. Stuff like that." The look on her face is almost guilty.

"Did she mention Ariel?"

"No." The word is drawn out a bit.

"When she asked you who your friends were, did you mention Ariel?" I ask, keeping my voice casual.

"I might have," she says in a way that makes me read it as a yes.

The counselor jumps in. "Ashleigh, if you did mention Ariel to the woman, it's not your fault that something happened to Ariel." She's trying to be helpful but I don't want her interfering.

Ashleigh bites her lip and her edge disappears; suddenly she looks very young. "When we were talking, I saw Ariel going back into school and I called out to her." She addresses her response to the counselor.

"Ashleigh," I say, drawing her attention back. "What did the woman say?" I cut a look at the counselor and I hope her eagle eye can read my request for her to stay silent.

"She said she enjoyed talking to us and that she'd see us again soon." The fear is back in her face. "Do you think that she's going to come to the school again?"

"You don't have to worry about that," Steve assures her. "We are going to have a real policewoman here at the school for a while."

I applaud Steve's motivation for saying this but am irritated that now he has broken the tempo of the interview.

"After she said that," I say, "what did she do?"

"She left. She walked out of the side gate and got into her car and drove off."

Steve jots a reminder in his notepad.

"What type of car was it?"

She shrugs. "It was black."

"Did you see the license plate?"

She shakes her head three times.

"You're being really helpful Ashleigh. I just need to ask you a couple more questions."

"OK." She manages a wan smile.

"Ariel told you that she didn't want to be on *Canada's Littlest Beauty*, didn't she?"

She nods and Steve cuts a sharp look at me. He's going to be ticked off that I didn't tell him about this earlier.

"Can you tell me why?"

"It was her Mom. She made Ariel work so hard and practice her dancing and singing and gymnastics, like all the time. Ariel had lessons every Saturday and Sunday and she had to travel all over to those stupid shows. Can you believe she had to fly to Toronto for like one performance. She hated it but her Mom wouldn't listen to her."

"Ellie said that you told Ariel to stand up to her Mom."

"She did too. Her Mom got so mad. She said Ariel could

never talk to me again. She even came to the school and complained about me. Her Mom hated me anyway."

Out of the corner of my eye, I see that the counselor is about to speak again. I give her a hard look and hold up my index finger to silence her. I see her inner debate going on.

I turn back to Ashleigh and smile, hoping that she didn't catch the look I gave her teacher. "Why?"

"'Cause my parents aren't rich like hers." That rings true.

"Now Ash—" her counselor starts to speak

I speak over her. "I think you're a really good friend to Ariel," I say.

She smiles.

"Did she say anything about any of the people who worked on the show? Was there anyone who frightened her or made her feel uncomfortable?"

"She said some of the other kids on the show were mean… and their Moms." I can validate that. In the episode I watched last night, some of the parents were brutal.

"What about the people from the TV company?"

She shrugs.

"Can you think of anything else that might help us find Ariel?" I ask.

She shakes her head.

"Just one last question. Apart from Megan and Kaylee, is there anyone else who Ariel might have talked to?"

"No. She didn't even tell *them* about wanting to stop doing *Canada's Littlest Beauty* because they thought it was sooooo cool to be on the show." Her young voice is laced with vitriol for Megan and Kaylee.

"OK, Ashleigh you've—"

"Oh, there was Justin."

"Who's Justin?" Not someone from school, St. Cecelia's is all girls.

"A boy," she giggles. I can hear the counselor's grunt of disapproval.

"Where does she know him from?"

"She met him on Facebook and they Messenger each other all the time. She showed me some of the messages, he's really nice but kinda shy."

Steve and I exchange looks. "Ariel had a cell phone?" I ask.

"Cellular telephones are not allowed on school property."

I turn on her. "That is not relevant to my interview, Mrs...?" I don't even know her name.

"O'Reardon. And it's Miss."

"Ms. O'Reardon," I say, "you are here for Ashleigh's protection, to guard her interests in the absence of a parent. I will thank you to keep any other comment to yourself during this interview." Suddenly, I remember I am a civilian now and I have a lot less official standing in this room than she does.

I turn back to Ashleigh with a smile and see that she is smiling too. Clearly she's not a member of Team O'Reardon.

"So, Ariel had a cell phone."

"Yes. It was an iPhone, she was so lucky."

Why in heaven's name didn't Rebecca Bradbury mention this to the police or, for that matter to me?

"Don't tell her Mom, she'll be mad," Ashleigh answers the unasked question.

"Where did she get it?"

"Justin gave it to her. His Dad works for a cell phone company."

"So she met Justin face-to-face?" I ask, just knowing the answer is not going to be the one I want to hear.

"No. He hid the phone in the hedge outside her house one night so she could pick it up next morning. She Messengered with him from her iPad to arrange it."

"Did they ever speak to each other on the phone?"

"I think so. But it was mainly text, Facebook and email. But I'm pretty sure she talked to him too." Her tone is matter-of-fact.

Hoping against hope I ask, "Do you know the number?"

She nods and recites the digits which Steve writes down. He nods at me and leaves the room.

"Did Ariel's parents know she had a Facebook page?"

"She had two. One her Mom set up using her real name and it was all about the stupid show. But the other one she set up herself; she called herself Ariel Notastar. Not a star, get it?"

I feel very old. Eight year-old girls can set themselves up on Facebook? I've only just learned how to do that. Ellie has a computer at my house and another at Sam's, I wonder...

Now's not the time for that issue.

I get out my iPhone and hand it to her. "Can you show me Ariel's Facebook pages?" I ask.

She taps away for a few seconds. "Here's her Mom's page." She hands it to me. I click on photos and see an array of pics of Ariel in the costumes she wears on the show. In many of them she is posing in overtly sexual ways and I wonder again how a mother can encourage, no, pressure her daughter to do this. It is like a pedophile's photo album. I remember the photo that Rebecca Bradbury gave me where she's been made to look like a teenager. I make a mental note to get Stammo to dig around on Facebook a bit.

"How about her own page?" I hand the phone back to Ashleigh just as Steve walks back in.

He shakes his head. Ariel's phone number turned up nothing useful... unless Steve is holding stuff back from me.

Ashleigh hands my phone back to me. It shows Ariel's own page. I click her profile, it says, "Doing stuff on a STUPID TV show."

I look at her timeline pictures and they are of Ariel behaving like any normal kid: hanging out with her friends; clowning around; just like millions of others.

I go to the friends section and scroll through. My stomach

does an uncomfortable flip as my other unasked question is answered. Ellie smiles out of the screen at me.

Then just below Ellie's picture is a Justin Brown, a good-looking boy, about ten years old. I show it to Ariel and she nods. "That's Justin."

"Have you ever met him face-to-face?" I ask. She shakes her head.

There is a knock on the door and a young woman enters. She is dressed in a steampunk style—her jacket is adorned with brass and silver gear wheels and levers and distorted, Dali-esque clock faces—and she gives me a flash-forward of what Ashleigh might look like in ten years' time. She nods at Steve and smiles at me.

Steve makes the introduction. "Ashleigh, this is Sarah. She is from our forensic unit." He sees the confusion on Ashleigh's face. "You know like *CSI* on TV." Nothing. Clearly Ashleigh's parents monitor her viewing, if not her computer use. "She is going to ask you some questions about that woman who was dressed like a police officer and she is going to try and make a picture of her on the computer. OK?"

She nods.

Steve and I make our exit and leave Sarah to work her magic with Ashleigh and the computer.

Steve's phone rings and I know from his end of the conversation that the news is not good.

"The phone?" I ask him.

"It was on a pay-as-you-go plan with Telus. The texts were to another pay-as-you-go and they have both been switched off since Friday afternoon. Unfortunately, Telus only keeps the actual messages on their servers for three days. We're a day late and a dollar short."

He is not pleased with what he has heard and, worse, it triggers a memory for him. "What was all that in there about *Canada's Littlest Beauty*?" he asks. "Have you been holding out on me again, Cal?"

Before I can answer, his phone rings again.

"Waters." He listens, looks at me and turns away, talking quietly.

Time to *carpe momentum*. I take off through the nearest door and head for my car. It's time to call Stammo and get him to use some of his computer skills.

13

CAL

I'm sorry, Mr. Radcliffe doesn't speak with private detectives," she says. Rather than resist, I just look at her, a slight smile playing about my lips. She has that self-assurance many beautiful women have; I enjoy watching it crumble under the steady pressure of my stare. She is not going to impede me from the pledge to find Ariel.

"What?" she says.

"I'm investigating the disappearance of one of the children who perform on your show. Are you sure Mr. Radcliffe doesn't want to help with that?" I ask.

Her face changes. It's either fear or disgust. "Who?" she says, "Who's disappeared?"

"If you had to guess, who do *you* think it would be?" I ask. I give her the look I've leveled at many suspects in many interview rooms.

"Me? I don't know. I'm just Mr. Radcliffe's personal assistant." Her voice has taken on a defensive tone. At this point I could just ask to see her boss and she would cave, but I have taken an illogical dislike to her.

"You're just his P.A.?" I say, my voice implying that she is lying to cover up a panoply of guilty deeds.

"Yes. Really. Listen, let me talk to Mr. Radcliffe again…"
She snatches the phone from its cradle. She gives me an unexpected smile and I feel a bit guilty about pressuring her.

Within two minutes, I am sitting on a leather chair in the office of Mr. Thomas Radcliffe, Executive Producer of *Canada's Littlest Beauty*.

The office is not nearly as lavish as I expected. The furniture is flashy but cheap and the general air of the place is one of style but not substance. Maybe this is one of the ways Vancouver, 'the Hollywood of the North', differs from the real item. Radcliffe doesn't fit with my preconceptions of a TV producer, either. He is casually dressed in jeans and a T-shirt with the show's logo; only his shoes look expensive. He looks more like a university student than the producer of a successful TV franchise. Then again, maybe I'm just assuming the show is successful.

He sits on the corner of his desk, holding my business card using the thumbs and index fingers of both hands. "So how can I help you Mr. Rogan?" he asks.

"Do you know that Ariel Bradbury has gone missing?" I ask.

I am almost sure that the shock on his face is genuine. "No," he says. "What happened? Did her mother throw her out for lacing her shoes wrong or something?"

Immediately he regrets his flippancy. "Sorry, I shouldn't have said that. It's just that… well… her mother is the most demanding woman I have ever met. She's brutal. It's what makes Ariel so right for this show. She's a nice girl and all, and has talent for sure, but it's her mother's wheeling, dealing and conniving that brings in the viewers. She is a piece of work, that woman." He shakes his head.

Despite my loathing for his show, I find myself liking Thomas Radcliffe. "Why do you think she is so obsessed with winning these beauty pageants?" I ask.

He gives a cynical snort. "I have no idea why any of the

mothers do it. For most of them, maybe it's because they're losers in life and they're living their dreams through their daughters. But Rebecca isn't like that. She's a successful woman and she's got more money than God. I have no idea why it matters to her." He shrugs. "She's giving me a lot of viewers though."

A question leaps into my mind. "Until I told you, you didn't know Ariel was missing, did you?"

He looks at me. He knows he's already answered this question. I detect a look of uncertainty.

He shakes his head.

Then I ask the question. "So didn't Rebecca call you and tell you Ariel wouldn't be available for filming this week?"

He frowns. He knows I'm trying to catch him in a lie.

"No, we're between seasons. The current series ends in June but we've already filmed all the episodes. We're not going to start filming the next season until next month."

"Were you planning to have Ariel back on the show next season," I ask.

"For sure. And Rebecca was very keen too. After Ariel failed to win the national contest in Toronto, Rebecca was furious. But she was determined to take a shot at it again next year. That woman…" He shakes his head.

"Were any of the other contestants' parents particularly upset at Ariel or her mother?"

"Only one."

"Upset enough to do anything to Ariel?"

He is not as shocked at the thought as I expected he might be. "No. This one girl, Tammy, had a real aggressive mother. She threw a lot of trash talk in Ariel's direction but Tammy ended up beating out Ariel in Toronto, so I don't see that she would have a reason to do anything… other than gloat."

"Was there anyone who might want to harm the show? Did you fire anyone recently?"

"Yeah. I fired a continuity girl. I found her using my

computer, going through some files. She was crap at her job anyway so it gave me a good excuse to can her."

"Anyone else?"

His face is expressionless for a moment. I watch his eyes. He's looking down to his left: having an internal debate. He rubs the side of his face... And he decides.

"No. Just the one."

Pause.

"You're sure?" I ask.

He gets up off the corner of the desk, walks around and sits in his chair.

"Yeah." He replies.

The certainty in his voice is forced. Boy, I'd like to play poker with this guy.

"Who was the other one you fired?"

He looks to his left. He's accessing a memory.

"No one." Even the forced certainty is gone.

"I don't believe you Mr. Radcliffe."

A flare of arrogance. "Who the fuck are you to tell—"

I stand up fast, plant my fists on his desk and lean over him. "Listen to me very carefully Mr. Radcliffe. I'm gonna say this once and once only."

I stare down at him.

"What?"

"I'm working closely with the police on this. If I walk out of here without an answer, I'm gonna call them. When they come to speak to you, they are going to want to know why you lied to me about this. They will probably want to question everyone on the show. Everyone, including all the contestants. They are going to subpoena files, tear this place apart and tear your life apart. You can avoid all that by telling me the truth right now."

Silence.

There is a worried look on his face.

More silence.

"Five seconds, Mr. Radcliffe."

I count to five, straighten up and turn toward the door praying that he doesn't call my bluff.

"OK, OK. I had to fire one of the sound guys."

I turn back and look at him… waiting…

He deflates. "Tammy's mother complained he was getting what she called 'too friendly' with the girls, touching them too much when he was putting on their mics. When I confronted him with it, he completely overreacted, got really abusive. We can't have anyone on the show that might become a liability, so I didn't want to take a chance with him. I fired his ass."

"You did the right thing getting him off the show." It never hurts to throw a bone to a witness who has given up some useful information.

He relaxes, gives a half smile and a nod.

Time to hit him again.

"So why did you just lie to me? Why did you try to cover up that you fired him from the show?"

I love the words 'cover up'—so much more emotive than 'hide'.

"I didn't," he protests but even he knows it's BS.

He stares at his hands for a moment and then looks me straight in the eye. "With Ariel missing, I didn't want to put the show in a bad light. I couldn't just tell you that one of my people had been accused of inappropriate behavior. It was probably a false accusation anyway." His explanation is reasonable and his voice is sincere… but I know he's lying.

"So what was this sound guy's name?" I ask.

"Listen. You can't tell him you got his name from me, OK."

"He won't have a clue." One good lie deserves another.

"It's Mark Traynor."

"Give me his personnel file."

He taps away at the keys of his computer for a while and

after a moment the printer on the credenza behind him starts whirring. He hands me the sheets it disgorges: personnel records for Mark Traynor, complete with photograph.

I thumb through the pages. It's got an address.

"D'you know where he works now?" I ask.

He shakes his head but when he sees the look in my eye, he says. "Yeah." He scribbles on a notepad and hands it to me. It's the name of a production company. "He's working on their latest movie."

"Thanks."

"Would you like Sherri Oliver's file too?" Radcliffe is being helpful now.

"Who's that?"

"The continuity girl I fired."

"Sure."

As he clicks at the keyboard, I ask him for a list of the parents on the show which he also supplies.

Back in my car, I look at the personnel records. Sherri Oliver, the continuity girl, is smiling out of the photo at me, she has dark hair in a ponytail and is kind of cute and wholesome looking. Mark Traynor, the sound guy, has a mop of black curly hair and wears nerdy-looking glasses.

I'm not hopeful. Neither of them appears like they are capable of kidnapping a child but looks are deceiving so I'll follow up with them anyway.

Who knows? Maybe this Traynor guy will pan out. And I got the info on him one step ahead of the VPD.

14

STAMMO

The drug squad had no information on Tyler, so I'm doing it the old-fashioned way. It feels good to be on the streets again. And on these streets, I fit right in. I roughed up some old clothes, got 'em dirty and now, sitting in my fucking wheelchair, I'm part of the landscape. I can just wheel myself around the downtown east side like any one of the hundreds of other wheelchair people who live here.

But despite all that, I can still feel the air of menace in the streets. It could explode at any time if anyone recognizes me as an ex-cop. But it's worth the risk. If I can find Tyler maybe I can get his Dad to help me find Matt.

I must'a talked to fifty street level dealers. When I could get their attention, they looked at the picture of Tyler. Most said, "Don't know him." A couple of 'em said, "Maybe I've seen him around." I figure among these guys, suspicious of everyone, a maybe-I've-seen-him-around is a positive ID. For what it's worth, I've handed out a lot of my business cards.

My arms are getting pretty tired doing all this wheeling but it feels kinda good. I don't get enough exercise in this goddamn chair. I'm gonna take a break and drop into Beanie's pub for a beer.

"You're Nick Stammo, ain't'cha?"

This cannot be good. I feel vulnerable in my chair.

It's one of the bouncers employed by Beanie's to keep the peace.

"Yeah," I say. No use denying it.

"Don't recognize me do ya?" he says.

I look into his face.

Then I remember.

"Hello Eddie. How's it hanging?"

"Pretty good." He seems quite friendly for a man I arrested a couple of times; second time sent him to prison too. "I hear you're not a cop no more."

"Yeah. I hear you're not dealing drugs no more."

He laughs.

"Nah. I was too low in the chain o' command to make any real money. My last time in prison, I got straight and when I got out, I went straight. Been working here ever since eh."

"Fancy a beer?" I ask him. "On me."

"I'd kill for one right now but I'm working eh."

"Some other time maybe."

I start to wheel in. Wait a minute.

"Hey Eddie," I call. He steps over to me and I show him the picture of Tyler Wilcox. "D'you know this guy?"

Eddie looks at the picture and it's clear he doesn't like what he sees. "Yeah. I know him. He works for the Bookman. Nasty piece of work."

"What makes you say he's a nasty piece of work?" Even I can hear the edge in my voice. Tyler was always a good little kid.

"Not the kid. He's just a newbie. It's the Bookman who's the nasty piece of work." He looks around furtively worried that some other ears might hear his comments and pass them on to the Bookman. Bookman must be heavy. The Eddie I remember was afraid of nothing.

"How come I've never heard of him?"

"He's fairly new in town but he's right up there. An enforcer. Always tooling about in that fancy great car of his."

"What sort of car?" Maybe I can track Tyler through this Bookman character. Someone in VPD will know about him.

A big smile comes to Eddie's face. "It's a beautiful set of wheels. It's a Shelby Mustang GT350. Blue and white. Goes like hell."

"Who does he work for?" I ask.

Eddie's face goes blank. "I dunno." It's a lie.

"Thanks man. I appreciate your help," I say. If I can just get him to open up a bit more... "Sure I can't buy you that beer?"

He licks his lips, on the edge of a decision.

"Nah, another time eh?"

"I'd like that. Hey look Eddie, if you think of anything, gimme a call, OK?" I give him one of my cards.

He slides the card into his pocket. "Sure." He thinks for a bit. "We never had this conversation, OK?"

"What conversation?"

He frowns and the words come out as a whisper. "About the Bookman." He looks at me and the penny drops. "Ooh... I get it. Yeah, right. What conversation?" He chuckles.

Eddie never was the sharpest knife in the drawer but he has taken me one step closer to finding Tyler Wilcox.

I hope so anyway. I gotta find him before he gets in too deep with whatever he's doing for the man who got Eddie so scared.

15

CAL

Bad news," Stammo's voice says into my earpiece. "What bad news, Nick?" I ask. *"The Bookman."* The Bookman? What the hell is he talking about? "I don't follow," I say.

"I just found out Tyler Wilcox has been hanging out with a guy known as the Bookman." I had almost forgotten about Nick's client from back East with the missing son. Ariel is my priority right now but I can't tell Nick that.

"OK."

"And I just had a chat with a buddy of mine from the drug squad."

"Uh-huh." I am only half listening as I weave my way through the midday traffic. My next interview may produce a major lead to finding Ariel and I want to stay ahead of my former colleagues.

"The Bookman is a new guy in town and guess who he works for?" I cut in front of a Lexus and earn a loud blast from its horn. I am not in the mood for guessing games.

"Who, Nick?" I try to keep the frustration out of my voice.

"Carlos Santiago."

Now he's got my attention. Santiago is probably the

73

biggest drug dealer in Canada and definitely one of the smartest in the world. He is Mr. Teflon: the VPD Drugs and Gangs squad and the RCMP have taken several runs at him but nothing sticks. Ostensibly he's a food importer and a venture capitalist. He has a mansion in Shaughnessy, a big estate in the Gulf Islands and a thirty-million-dollar yacht that he keeps at the marina in Yaletown: lots of expensive toys. He even pays taxes. They think he makes a big portion of his money transshipping drugs through Canada and into the United States. According to some sources, he's the third richest man in Canada. If Tyler Wilcox is mixed up with Santiago, it is not good news.

"What do you know about this Bookman character? Did you get a photo?" If we are going to find Tyler by tracking down the Bookman, we're going to need more solid intel on him than just the suspicion that has been worming its way through my mind.

"That's what's funny. VPD's got nothing on him. Zip. Nada. All they know is that he is from out of town. They don't even know where. They didn't even know he drives a Shelby GT350. I got us some brownie points by telling 'em. If we can get a picture of him, we'll be the golden boys." Stammo chuckles. He never did that when he was a cop. *"Anyways, I need you to help me track him down. ASAP."*

"I'm following up a lead on the Ariel Bradbury case, right now." My voice betrays my frustration.

Silence.

In the pause, I can't stop the dread I feel at the thought of being plunged back into the world of drugs that the Tyler case is about. I have to stay clear of that world.

The call may have dropped but I'm betting Nick is having an internal debate. He really wants to find Tyler but he also knows we are getting a really juicy fee on the Ariel case.

"Ninety percent chance that she's dead already," he says.

It's difficult to argue the statistics but I can't give up on her like that. "I've got to keep trying," I say.

"When will you be back in the office?" he asks.

"This afternoon."

He grunts.

"Nick, I need you to do some of your magic with the internet."

"OK… but on one condition."

My turn to grunt.

"I need you to spend this afternoon tracking down this Bookman guy." His words are coming fast. *"He's my only lead to Tyler and I—"*

"Nick, we are getting big bucks to trace Ariel, I can't just—"

"Cal, please. This kid is like my own. I really need to find him before something bad happens to him. I need you to use your druggie contacts on the street. Please."

He never calls me Cal.

And he sure as hell never begs for anything.

"OK, Nick." I hear his sigh of relief. "But I can't do it this afternoon. I have to pick Ellie up from school."

"Oh."

"I'll do it tomorrow, I promise."

"OK. But no excuses tomorrow, promise?"

"Yeah, for sure. But I need you to do some digging on the internet."

I take his grunt for agreement. I tell him about Justin Brown, the kid who gave Ariel the cell phone and I can tell from his voice that he is going to rise to the challenge.

It's a win-win.

So why does it feel like a lose-lose?

———

HE STEPS out from between two trucks and our eyes meet.

"Are you Mark Traynor?"

"Who wants to know?" There is an undertone of aggression in his voice.

He pushes his glasses up to the bridge of his nose.

"I want to ask you about why Thomas Radcliffe fired you," I say.

Puzzlement for a beat, followed by aggression again.

"Fuck you." The geeky look from his photo is absent. Despite what Sam may say, the camera *does* lie.

I grab the front of his AC-DC T-shirt and yank him toward me. Our noses are almost touching. This is one of the advantages of no longer being a cop. "Unless you answer some questions my friend, it's *you* who will be well and truly fucked."

Now we're back to fear. He looks around. The film set is on the library forecourt on Robson Street. All his colleagues are busy and any passers-by will assume that we are actors rehearsing—Vancouverites are blasé about all the filming that goes on around them.

"I repeat: why did Thomas Radcliffe fire you?"

"He didn—" He cuts himself off.

"Are you telling me he didn't fire you?" I insert a note of incredulity into my voice.

"Yes… Well, no…"

"Which is it?"

"It's complicated."

I let go of his T-shirt and he takes a step backward, adjusting his glasses again. His eyes are strange. One is greenish and the other brown.

"Why don't you explain it to me, Mark." Mr. Reasonable, that's me.

"I don't have to explain anything." Sullen.

Now I focus in on his face and hit him with both barrels.

"You get fired for feeling up little girls…" I see a flash of

76

anger, "and then one of those little girls gets kidnapped. Maybe you could explain that one to me Mark?"

The anger is replaced by surprise. He couldn't fake that, even if he worked on the other side of the cameras. He has no idea.

"Who got kidnapped?" he asks.

"It doesn't matter." Mark Traynor is not a suspect. Shame. I would have loved to nail the little worm.

A hard look comes into his eye. "How d'you find out I work here?" he asks.

My first impulse is to tell him that I tracked him down through the production company whose name Radcliffe gave me.

But then I wonder why he's asking.

"How d'you think?" I give him a knowing smile.

"That fucker Radcliffe," he says, as much to himself as to me.

"Why would Radcliffe tell me where you worked?"

"Did *he* tell you that bitch of a mother accused me of touching the girls?" he answers my question with one of his own.

"Yeah. Told me that was why he fired you."

His lips are drawn into a tight line.

"He's a fuckin' liar. First, I never touched any of those girls and he knows it. That's just sick. Second he didn't fire me. In fact, he pulled a few strings to get me this job."

I hope I have the right tone of mockery in my voice. "Why would he do that?"

"To shut me up, of course."

"About what?"

He realizes he has said too much.

"About what?" I step closer to him.

Silence. He pushes his glasses up his nose again. Having eyes of differing colors gives him a kind of crazy look.

He doesn't know who I am, so I take a shot. "Either you

tell me now or you can come with me to the Cambie Street police station and explain it there."

His eyes do the trapped-animal routine.

It could go either way. If he calls my bluff, that's it.

"Listen, Mark. You don't owe Radcliffe anything. He told me he saw you molesting those girls and fired you. He's trying to put this whole thing on you. Unless you can give me a good reason, I'm going to have to take you in for questioning."

"OK," he says.

He called my bluff. Now what do I do?

"OK. You're right. I don't owe that fucker anything."

Oh.

"So what really happened?" I ask.

"That little brat, Tammy, told her bitch of a mother I touched her when I put on her mic. It was a total lie. I'm not like that." Something tells me that he is a bit like that, maybe a lot like that. I wonder if the relationship with Thomas Radcliffe is more than just business. "Anyways, the mother screams at Radcliffe, tells him I've been feeling up all the girls. That show was Radcliffe's big break. He's not going to let anything spoil it for him. So he fires me to shut her up." He uses his fingers to make quotes when he says the word 'fires'. "Only he knows he can't fire me." A sly look comes into his eyes.

"Why's that?" I ask.

"Let's say that I know something that he wouldn't want anyone involved with *Canada's Littlest Beauty* to know."

"And what's that?"

He bites his lip, unsure.

"It's him or you, Mark."

He nods.

"Way back, when he first started in the business, he made a few porno flicks. I know 'cos I worked as a gaffer on them. When I heard he was cleaning up with *Beauty*, I got him to get me a job on the set. With what I knew, he couldn't refuse. So when that bitch mother got him to fire me, I made him give me a good whack of severance pay *and* get me a better job… or else."

It seems like a reasonable story, except…

"I dunno, Mark. These days, half the movies you see could be called porn. Would he really need to buy your silence?"

A very creepy look morphs onto his bespectacled face.

"He would if the stars of his early films were in grade seven at the time."

16

STAMMO

"Hell on wheels! You've done good, Rogan." He has too; twenty-four hours after his lunch with Rebecca Bradbury and he's uncovered a possible pedophile connected to her kid.

"Yeah, I suppose. But when we got the case she'd been missing for almost four days. Time's running out"

"You'd have thought she'd have checked out this Radcliffe character before putting her daughter on his TV show."

His eyes narrow. "What's stranger still is that she never told me about the show. I found out from Ellie last night. It doesn't make any sense to me. I'm going straight from here to talk to Rebecca about it. Anyway, were you able to find any answers for me?"

"Yeah, but first I need to know if you have told Steve all this about Radcliffe and his sound guy."

"I will tell him but I just need—"

"No way, Rogan! You need to tell him right now. He needs to pick up Radcliffe and interrogate the fuck out of him."

"But it's just on the word of this sound guy, Traynor. It's not—"

"Doesn't matter. You've still gotta tell him. Better yet, when we're finished here, I'm gonna tell him."

"OK, OK. But just tell me what did you find out about this Justin kid."

He's not going to like one of the answers for sure. "So, do you want the good news or the bad news?" I ask.

"There's good news?"

"I dug into Justin's Facebook." That brings the old spark back to Rogan's eyes. "I'm pretty sure that he's not a kid. I think he's an adult grooming kids. I read a bunch of his posts and he asks the girls questions that get more and more personal. He's clever. There's nothing indecent just kinda innuendo. That girl Ariel really went for it. She spent a lot of time complaining about her Mom and he just played her like a fiddle. Maybe 'Justin' is this Radcliffe guy."

"Well done, Nick, I had an idea he wasn't a real kid because no one has seen him face-to-face or talked to him. You might be right about Radcliffe too. Did you get anything else?"

"Oh yeah, the bad news." I nod and make him wait for it. Just as I spot he's about to burst, "Ariel's not the only one."

Rogan's eyes are saucers now. I gotta say, I like it when I know something he doesn't. "About nine months ago, there was a kid named Olivia, same age as Ariel. She had a big conversation with 'Justin' then it suddenly stopped. So I checked the news for nine months ago. There was a girl named Olivia Norton went missing in Coquitlam. She's never been found."

"My God." He thinks for a bit. "Do you think we should tell the VPD and the Coquitlam RCMP?"

"Already done."

A look of annoyance passes across his face. "Nick, we need to discuss these things first before we just pass information on. It makes better financial sense for us to be able to keep ahead of the police investigation. It gives us an edge, right?"

"Bull*shit*, Rogan," now I'm mad. "You just need to prove that you're better than them. You're just using the money angle to try and play me. We *cannot* keep material evidence from them. One, it's against the law and two, we need to keep 'em on our side."

He sighs. "Yeah, I suppose. But we're a team now and—"

"I know and teammates listen to each other, don't they?" Before he can answer, I barrel on, "I got something else. I've been studying up on some networking stuff recently and I was able to track down Justin's IP address." I can't help grinning at the look on his face. Respect, I think they call it.

"What, you hacked Facebook?" he says.

"No. I'm not that good. But I did Messenger him, pretending to be a friend of Ariel's. I used the name, Lucy. I kinda played him a bit and I got him to go to a website I set up telling him I had a naked picture posted there. I used the website to get his IP address. Bingo."

"You're the man Nick." He reaches across the table and gives me a fist bump. "Do you have a physical location?"

"Yeah, of course."

Before I can go on, he's on his feet. "Well done, Nick." He pumps his fist in the air. Such a simple thing and I should feel great at his reaction but all I can think is that I will never be able to jump to my feet again. I feel my hand tighten on the arm of my wheelchair.

He looks at me and he knows. Looking a bit sheepish, he sits down again.

"Don't get too excited," I say. "The bad news is that the IP address is for an internet cafe on Salt Spring Island. He must go there every afternoon at three-thirty. Just about the time the girls are coming out of school. I called 'em. No CCTV in the place. Girl who answered the phone was a bit of an airhead so I don't think it's gonna go anywhere."

"That's great Nick. You know what? I'm going to take the ferry over there and talk to the staff. Maybe there are some CCTV cameras nearby. We could—"

"No need."

"What do you mean? It's a great lea—"

"I already talked to a buddy of mine who's at the RCMP detachment on the island. He's gonna do it and let me know."

"Nick…" His voice trails off. He doesn't want to fight our second favorite battle all over again. "You said there were two things."

Before I can tell him the really bad news, my phone rings.

"Nick Stammo."

"It's Eddie, Mr. Stammo." My buddy from Beanie's pub.

"Hi, Eddie. What's up?"

"You said you were trying to find that kid who hangs out with the Bookman."

"That's right, Eddie."

"Yeah, well a buddy of mine knows him eh."

"That's great Eddie, do you know where I can find him?"

"Yeah, I do. My buddy says every day, around midday, on Hastings outside the Backpackers. Him and the Bookman show up regular as clockwork, eh."

The Backpackers is a flophouse known for drug dealing.

"Well done Eddie. Thanks, I owe ya one."

A chuckle. *"Yeah you do, Mr. Stammo."*

Rogan sees the big grin on my face as I hang up.

"Got a lead to Tyler?"

I tell him the details.

"Do you want me to go with you?" he asks.

I turn it over in my mind.

"To tell you the truth, Rogan, a big part of me wants you there. But I don't want to spook Tyler with an unfamiliar face. He knows me and I can probably get him to talk to me just one-on-one."

He nods. He's relieved. He wants to get on with the Ariel case.

But now I've gotta tell him the really bad news about the Justin 'kid'.

———

ROGAN'S RUSHED off to see Rebecca Bradbury and I've told Steve all about Radcliffe and Traynor. He's going to pick Radcliffe up for questioning.

It's almost six back east and he picks up on the third ring. *"Bob Wilcox."*

"Hi Bob, it's Nick."

A silence then one word, spoken cautiously. *"News?"*

"Yes. First thing, Tyler's alive and well." I hear the sigh of relief over two thousand seven hundred and thirty miles of telephone wire. "But he's fallen in with a drug gang. I won't mince words here Bob, these are pretty bad people."

He groans. *"Is there anything you can do Nick?"*

"Possibly. I'm gonna try and see him tonight, see if I can get some time with him and talk some sense into him."

"Thanks Nick. Fact is, I don't know how to thank you enough."

"Don't thank me yet. Thank me when you get him back."

"Nick, I could pay you y'know."

"No way, Bob. I wouldn't take yer money. We go too far back." He's silent so I add, "There is one thing you could maybe do for me."

"Sure Nick, anything."

I hesitate, unsure. Do I really want to know? I wobble on the edge, undecided. Then, "Nah, forget it. You've got enough on your mind worrying about Tyler."

"Are you sure, Nick? I'd be happy to do anything."

"No, it's alright. I'll call you again after I've spoken with Tyler."

"OK, Nick. Thanks."

We hang up. I chickened out. But I must remember to pay some money into the company account. I told Rogan this was a paying case.

17

CAL

This is not acceptable Mr. Rogan. When I hired you, I asked you to call me every evening to report back to me on your progress. You did not call me last night and suddenly here you are on my doorstep, uninvited, on Wednesday afternoon."

Rebecca Bradbury is not a happy camper. But then again, nor am I.

"Mrs. Bradbury, I need to ask you some questions, especially about why you didn't tell me of Ariel's involvement in *Canada's Littlest Beauty*. Unless you can be honest with me, you are wasting your money and my time, so, if you want me to continue this investigation, we need to talk. Now." It's a bluff. Even if she fired me right now, I couldn't let go of this case.

She holds me in her stare for a while before opening the door enough to let me in.

Without a word, she leads me into a living room off the main lobby.

The house is both huge and beautiful. Typical Shaughnessy old money. Worth ten million at the very least.

"Please sit down."

She picks up a telephone. It has no buttons or controls. "Tea for two in the sitting room please Edna." She hangs up.

I hate tea.

Before she can sit down, I take the offensive. "Why didn't you tell me about Ariel being a contestant in that show."

"I didn't see it as being relevant," she says and I can tell she genuinely believes this.

"Then it will interest you to know that the producer of the show spent the early part of his career making kiddy-porn movies. Not only that, he had to fire one of the crew for allegedly touching some of the contestants inappropriately."

Her face has gone pale. "I can't believe th—"

"Whether you believe it or not is immaterial. It's true. If you had told me about the show, I would be twenty-four hours ahead of where I am now."

Her face is stricken.

"Oh my God, what have I done?" she whispers.

"Why ever did you put her on that show?" My voice is gentle now.

She is silent for a while. A long while. I match her silence, intuitively knowing that she is going to tell me something worth knowing.

"I wanted to give her something I never had."

I look around the room and recall the words of Thomas Radcliffe the producer. *She's got more money than God.* "What could that possibly be?" I ask.

She takes a deep breath.

"I don't expect you to understand this but my entire life has been controlled by others... by men. My father decided what school I should go to, then what university and what I should study and whom I should marry. Before his death, Daddy transferred the bulk of his wealth—tens of millions of dollars I might add—into my husband's merchant bank and, although I own this house and have a very generous trust

ROBERT P. FRENCH

fund, Ariel's future will be very much controlled by *her* father.

"I wanted her to have a certain level of independence."

"I'm not sure I understand."

"I wanted Ariel to be in a position where she could have her own money with the ability to earn more."

"Did *Canada's Littlest Beauty* pay her?"

"No, of course not." She is irritated at my question. "Ariel is a bright girl but not at all academic. She was never going to excel intellectually. But she *is* beautiful and talented. I thought that if she could win the show's talent competition she would be able to get an agent and start doing some movie or TV roles or perhaps some serious modeling. She would be able to earn a great deal of her own money and make her own decisions." A look of infinite sadness has descended onto her face. "I wanted her to be what *she* wanted to be, not what her father wanted."

Or what you wanted her to be, I think. I manage to avoid volunteering that in my interview with Ashleigh, she told me about Ariel's hatred of the show; instead I ask, "What would you have been, given the choice, Mrs. Bradbury?"

No hesitation. "A journalist." Not what I would have expected.

"Ariel's been missing for five days now. Are you sure you've not received any ransom demand?"

"No. I wish I had. At least I would be able to *do* something."

I think she's telling the truth.

"Any kidnapper would contact my husband. *He* controls the family fortune." There's bitterness in the words.

I get the feeling she is really trying to convince me.

"If you do receive a demand, call me immediately. Don't try and go it alone. Taking the law into your own hands can only lead to bad things."

She nods.

She gives me the names and contact information for Ariel's dancing and singing teachers, both elderly women so I'm not holding my breath. I quiz her for a while about the show and the people in it but she has nothing of interest to offer and I can't rid my mind of the thought of how poor this rich woman is.

18

CAL

Ellie's sitting beside me looking out the car window. I mull over Stammo's bombshell and how to deal with it. Well… I guess there's no time like the present.

"Ell, Mommy said I could pick you up from school today because I need to talk to you about something."

"OK." She sounds unsure.

"I see you're on Facebook now."

"Yes?" The word is drawn out and there is a question in the tone.

"Does Mommy know about it?"

"Not really." Now there is a small tone of defensiveness in her voice. I need to tread carefully, pre-teen rebellion is not what I want right now.

"It's pretty cool. Did you set it up yourself?"

"Yes, Daddy." Now she's amused. "It's not difficult you know. All my friends have one."

"Would you show me how to do it," I ask.

"Sure." She laughs.

"Maybe we could do it this evening."

"OK."

Pause.

We stop for a traffic light.

"Ell, you know that I am working on the disappearance of Ariel Bradbury." Out of the corner of my eye, I see her nod. "Well Mr. Stammo has been checking up on some stuff and he discovered that Ariel had a Facebook friend named Justin."

"Oh yeah, I know. Justin's nice."

"The thing is Ell, when Mr. Stammo looked at Justin's Facebook, he found a lot of posts between you and Justin."

Pause.

"Did he show them to you?"

"Yes."

Pause.

"I thought they were private."

"Sweetie, nothing on the internet is private."

"Oh."

The lights change and I accelerate away.

"Does Mommy know?" she asks.

"No... Do you think I should tell her?"

Pause.

I glance at her and she shrugs.

"Sweetie, there's something you need to know. Justin doesn't exist."

"Don't be silly, Daddy. Of course he exists."

"Ell, Mr. Stammo and I and the police, we all believe that Justin is not a boy. We think he's a man pretending to be Justin. We think he kidnapped Ariel and another girl."

"No, you're wrong Daddy. He's definitely a boy."

"Ellie, he's not—" I stop myself. Confrontation is not going to work here. "Sorry. Maybe I'm wrong. But I need to know why you're so sure he's really a boy?"

"His voice."

"Have you met him face-to-face?"

"No, but..." she cuts herself off.

A chill slithers down my spine. I pull the Healey over to the side of the road and shut off the engine.

I turn in the seat toward her. "Sweetie, I think you need to tell me."

"I spoke to him on the phone." Her voice is quiet, her chin on her chest.

"When did you talk to him?"

"Yesterday."

"When yesterday?"

"He called me in the afternoon."

"On Mom's phone?"

Tiny voice, "No."

The chill slithers from my spine to my gut.

"Did he give you a phone, Ell?"

Almost a whisper. "Yes."

———

SAM IS NOT happy to be here. She has visited my apartment only once in the almost two years since I moved in. But it's more than that. It's the reason I asked her here. I gave her a brief synopsis over the phone.

We are sitting around my dining table. The phone that Ellie used to communicate with Justin is sitting in the middle. It feels more like a bomb than a phone.

"So Ell, you have to understand something about Justin," I say gently. "I know you think he is who he says he is, but he isn't."

"But he *is* Daddy. I've *spoken* to him."

"No sweetie, you spoke to a boy on the phone but he was only saying what an adult told him to say. He wasn't Justin."

"You're wrong," Ellie insists. "He was just talking normally. There was no one in the background telling him—"

"For heaven's sake Ellie," Sam breaks in, "listen to your father. You cannot have any further contact with this person. Do you understand?"

Sam's tone washes a stubborn look onto Ellie's face. Damn. I don't want her on the defensive.

"Do you understand?" Sam has added a couple of decibels.

"Yes." In contrast, it's barely more than a whisper.

"We're not mad at you, sweetie," I intercede. "We're just really worried." Out of the corner of my eye, I see Sam deflate a little. "You see, just after Ariel started talking to Justin was when she disappeared. The police and I believe that the people controlling Justin were responsible for her disappearance."

"You keep *saying* that but when I talked to him we just chatted. If someone was telling him what to say I would have heard them."

"Listen, Ell, you just have to trust us on this. Do you promise to have no further contact with Justin?"

Her "OK" doesn't sound very convincing.

Sam jumps in with, "Daddy's going to give this phone to the police and I'm going to delete your Facebook history."

"OK." She says it casually; she doesn't sound as angry as I would have expected.

"What's your password?" Sam asks.

"ellesbellsrogan," she says with a shrug. Oh. A question springs to my lips but I bite it back.

"OK. I am going to delete it when I get home. For a start, you have to be thirteen to have a Facebook page. Did you know that?"

Again with the shrug.

"So you lied about your age when you signed up?"

Ellie emits a tiny, "Yes."

Sam is in full swing now, it's rare for her to be so angry. "There will definitely be consequences for you Ell—" she stops, frowning. "Don't you have to have an email address to open a Facebook account?"

Ellie looks crestfallen. She nods.

Sam extracts her email address and password and is about to start another tirade but before she can get going I hold up my hand. I don't want to pressure Ellie this much. I want her to know that she can always come and talk to us *without* pressure, so I deflect, "Why don't we have dinner? It would be great if you could stay Sam."

She looks hard at me but I can't read her expression. She doesn't respond for a beat and I realize I'm holding my breath for her answer. Then she says, "Thanks for the offer but I can't. I'm going out tonight and I have to get ready. I need Ellie home by six-thirty at the latest. My neighbor Cora is going to babysit. Plus I need to get home and on my computer so I can remove Ellie's digital footprint."

"OK." She catches the disappointment in my voice but she doesn't relent; if anything it seems to make her more angry.

"And don't forget that Friday is a Pro-D day at her school and you said that you would take her from noon on. I really need you to do that as I have an appointment I *have* to go to." Her voice has taken on an edge of irritation.

She gives Ell a kiss and then leaves.

Now that Sam has gone, I can ask the question I wanted to ask earlier. "Ell, I'm going to make hamburgers now. Why don't you come into the kitchen and sit with me while I cook."

"Sure. Can I help?"

"Absolutely."

While she perches on a stool at the breakfast counter, I get olive oil, vinegar, honey and an empty jam jar. I place them in front of her and ask her to make the salad dressing, one of her favorite jobs.

As I putter around getting the ingredients together I say, "I'm not as strict as Mommy on the social media stuff." I glance over to see if there is a reaction but she seems focused on pouring the oil into the jar, her tongue peeking out from the side of her mouth. I putter some more. "So I'm guessing that Facebook isn't your only one." Out of the corner of my eye I see her finish pouring the oil and put the bottle on the countertop. I avoid looking directly at her and put the ground beef into a mixing bowl, followed by the breadcrumbs and garlic powder. I give her time. I grind pepper onto the mixture and see her pick up the balsamic vinegar bottle.

As she starts to pour it she says, "I've got Instagram too."

"Any others?"

"No."

"Are you and Justin friends on Instagram?"

"I follow him and he follows me."

I don't like the idea that is forming in my mind.

"So, in Instagram, can you send private messages to people?"

"Well duh!"

"Do you ever message with Justin?"

"Only on Facebook." She picks up the honey bottle and I start to knead the hamburger ingredients together.

"But you could message him on Instagram?"

She digests this for a while. "Are you going to stop me using Instagram?"

"I need to think about that."

And I need to think about whether I dare use my daughter to lure a predator from his lair.

————

I HAVE to consider my next step in the search for Ariel. Ellie has eaten and is watching a Simpsons rerun on TV. Sam and I agreed that she could only watch it with adult supervision but it's not getting my full attention. Ellie's conviction that Justin is really a kid has got me worried. Is the kidnapper using an actual kid to front for him? His son maybe or perhaps a kid whom he has kidnapped and forced to do the grooming for him. The latter is unlikely and a quick call to

Steve at VPD has confirmed that there are no recently missing young boys. Mark Traynor's information about Thomas Radcliffe's kiddy-porn background keeps forcing its way to the front of my head. Is Radcliffe the kidnapper? If so how can I prove it? Maybe if I grill him about it, he'll give something away. Maybe.

A google search for Thomas Radcliffe turns up his production company's website and on the About page there is a picture of him. I copy the image and paste it into a WORD doc and click Print. His picture goes into my file.

There's an advert on the TV.

"Ell, come over here and have a look at this picture, please."

She walks over and for a second I see that although she is not yet nine, she is going to grow into a beautiful woman. I cringe at the thought that some pervert, hiding behind the identity of a ten-year-old boy, is looking at her as a sex object.

"What is it Daddy?"

I take Radcliffe's photo from the top of the small stack of papers in my Ariel Bradbury file.

"Do you recognize this man?"

She looks carefully at the smiling face.

"Is he the man who kidnapped Ariel?"

"He's a suspect, for sure."

She continues looking for a couple of seconds.

"I don't think I've ever seen him before."

I pick up Mark Traynor's photo. "How about him?"

She shakes her head. "No."

As I put his picture down, I notice that Ellie's eyes are glued to the file. There is real fear in them. My spine is electrified. I have never seen her so terrified.

"What is it sweetie?" I ask as calmly as I can.

Her finger is trembling as she reaches out and touches the photo of Sherri Oliver, the continuity girl Thomas Radcliffe fired for snooping into his computer.

"That's just someone who worked on *Canada's Littlest Beauty*," I say to reassure her.

"No she's not!" she shouts. "She's that policewoman who was at school the day Ariel went missing."

In the shocked silence, I hear Bart Simpson's voice. *"You're the man, Homer."*

Apart from Ariel, Ellie is the only person, as far as I know, who has ever spoken to the boy named Justin…

And it all falls into place.

A wave of relief washes over me as I realize I no longer have to consider Ellie as bait, then a wave of guilt that I even considered it.

19

SAM

I stop applying the eyeliner and look more closely at my face in the mirror. I'm a bit behind. Deleting Ellie's Facebook account took longer than I thought it would. At least the anger has subsided and I feel guilty for shouting at Ellie the way I did. But I'm still mad at Cal. He didn't seem to mind about the Facebook thing *and* I think he's holding something back.

A couple of the lines around my eyes look more pronounced but I don't think I look thirty-seven. Do I? Almost thirty-eight. I met Cal what, fourteen years ago now. It was our wedding anniversary last week; neither of us remembered it. It's rather sad. Oh, damn you Cal, why do I always think about you when…

Stop. I'm too excited to dwell on things like that. I get to work with my new client tonight. This is a breakthrough for me. Not only have I got a new photography client but he is a high profile client *and* I am going to redesign his website. This is going to look great on my portfolio and will clinch the deal with—

"Mommy, I'm home from Daddy's and Mrs. Hunt is here," Ellie bursts into the bathroom. She loves being babysat by the best neighbor I have ever had. Cora is wonderful with her even if she does spoil her with too much chocolate.

"That's great, my lovely girl. Tell her I'm getting ready and I'll be down in a minute, OK?"

"'K." The whirlwind whooshes out of the bathroom.

I'd better get ready faster.

Cal clearly isn't interested in getting back together, despite what happened in the kitchen last year. When he was here yesterday evening and we were talking about it, he was just about to tell me why he didn't want for us to get back together and, thank heavens, Ellie cut him off with her dance performance. I was so glad that I didn't have to hear him tell me that he doesn't love me anymore. Stop Sam! If I keep thinking about this, I'll ruin my makeup. I couldn't get back with Cal anyway. His job has put Ellie and me in danger more than once plus he could slip back into drugs at any time. Time for a change of subject.

As I finish my eyeliner, I think about my new client. He's really rather good looking and he's not married, according to Facebook anyway. At our last meeting he seemed slightly flirtatious. I would definitely go out with him if he asked me.

I reach for my old favorite perfume. Cal loves— No! Time for a change. I look in my drawer and find the sampler of Liquid Cashmere I got from Sephora. New man, new perfume. But maybe I'm getting ahead of myself.

Hell no. Maybe I'll ask him out.

Suddenly my feelings are in a maelstrom. Hating myself for doing it, I put the Liquid Cashmere back in the drawer.

20

CAL

I am stationed just inside the entrance to the ballroom at the Waterfront Hotel, scrutinizing the faces of people attending the debate between Lucas Corliss and his opponent, the incumbent, Edward Perot. And I really don't want to be here. I need to hunt down Sherri Oliver. I'm betting either Radcliffe or Traynor or both of them are working with her. And I'm stuck here. Right now Steve might be picking up Radcliffe or Traynor for interrogation and will squeeze enough information out of one of them to beat me to finding Ariel. The thought ratchets up my frustration.

As people stream in, I search my memories for faces connected with the drug world. It is boring work and I suspect unnecessary. Whichever drug gang was responsible for the attempt on Corliss' life on Monday is unlikely to make a second attempt with all the security for this debate. The size of the team from Arnold's security firm has been doubled; Ian Peake has his guys out in force, recognizable by their hard looks and discreet earpieces. There are also several uniformed VPD members.

Because of my part in foiling the assassination attempt on Sunday, Lucas Corliss has insisted that Stammo Rogan Investigations be paid for my presence here. Although that pleases Stammo, I don't want to be here. Right now I regret leaving the VPD. If I were still there, I would be working full time on tracking down Ariel's kidnappers before the case becomes a murder investigation. I've been on the case for thirty hours and there is no clear path to who took Ariel. Every minute here makes her case a minute colder.

Stammo seems to be making some strides on the Tyler case. Tyler's connection with this Bookman character is big and more than a little scary. Tyler is playing in the big leagues which I'm guessing are way over his head.

"You OK, Cal?" says a voice in my ear. I look around and see Ian Peake twenty yards along the hallway, his hand to his mouth, disguising the fact that he is talking into the mic in his sleeve. I nod at him but notice the flush suffusing my cheeks. I just zoned out thinking about the Ariel and Tyler cases and he spotted that I wasn't paying attention to the job at hand.

I scan the elegant room with its crystal chandeliers and rich carpeting, looking for recent entrants whom I might have missed. No familiar faces.

I return my eyes to the lineup of people waiting to be checked over by the uniformed security guards before they enter the ballroom and I immediately recognize a face.

What is he doing here?

Then I make the connection. When I met with Ariel's father, Dave Bradbury, yesterday afternoon, his face looked familiar. I now know why. He was one of the four businessmen who barged through the doors of the gym two nights ago just before we took down the would-be assassins. He must be a supporter of Larry Corliss. If so, that's got to be good news for the former Mayor; politicians always need supporters with deep pockets.

I really want to go and talk to him to find out if he has received any blackmail demands but my instincts hold me back.

I watch him as a security guy waves a metal detector around his torso. He smiles and swaps a joke with the guard. No one would ever know from his demeanor that his daughter has been kidnapped. I would be beside myself if it were Ellie. Why is he not at home waiting for news? Where is the man who was almost in tears when I spoke with him?

A very unpleasant feeling is stirring in my gut.

Then I smell Coco.

"Hi Cal. What are you doing here?"

Sam.

"Hi Sam." Relief, surprise and pleasure paint a huge smile on my face. "I'm part of the security team, but more to the point, what are you doing here? When you said you had an appointment, I had no idea it would be here."

"My job," she grins. "I just got a big commission to do publicity photos."

I notice that she has the suitcase-on-wheels in which she keeps her camera equipment. "That's great, Sam. Did Arnold set you up with Larry Corliss?"

"No, Cal." A slight edge has slipped into her tone. "I managed to get this job all by myself."

"I didn't mean—"

"And it's not for Corliss."

"Perot?" The edge is in my voice now.

"Problem, Cal?" Ian Peake's tone tells me he is really saying I should be keeping my attention on the job for which I am being paid, not talking to beautiful women. His message elicits equal parts of guilt at dropping the ball and frustration that I have to stop this conversation with Sam.

I raise my left hand to scratch my temple and speak into the microphone. "No problem. Sorry, Ian."

I drop my hand. "Sorry, Sam. I have to pay attention to the people coming in."

I smile.

She doesn't.

As she takes off with her suitcase in tow, I notice her limp is more pronounced than usual and she is walking with the aid of a cane.

I turn my attention back to the people in the hallway. Edward Perot is coming through security. The guard has been briefed on who he is and signals him to go on in but Perot declines and has the guard pass the metal detector over him. I'm impressed. Politicians usually go for the special treatment; I like that Perot doesn't make a big deal of his status here.

Perot is talking to a woman who also impresses me. Alexis works for the hotel and has organized this event. She's cute too. She gave Ian's team and me a tour of the hotel so that we could familiarize ourselves with the layout.

People are gathering around Perot and shaking hands. One of them is David Bradbury. Shame. I was hoping his money would be on Corliss.

Next is a vaguely familiar-looking face. He is in his twenties and well dressed in business-casual. The clothes look expensive. As he passes security I can see his feet. He is wearing what look like snakeskin boots: flashy but expensive; it would be typical of someone rising fast in the hierarchy of a drug gang. And he has the look: a quiet yet unmistakable aura of menace. I try to remember where I have seen him before. Was he in the same gang as Goliath, the man Ian Peake shot during the Corliss event two days ago? His eyes are focused on someone and I follow his gaze to… Sam.

I rub my nose. "Guy in the black jacket and boots looks familiar and not in a good way," I say into the mic. "Keep someone close to him."

"Got it." He can hear the urgency in my voice.

I look over toward Ian. He is talking to one of his people, the one who helped take down the couple with the phony baby.

I turn back to the guy in the boots. He is no longer looking at Sam, thank God. Maybe he was just looking at her because she's beautiful. Maybe. He takes a seat close to the stage and starts tapping at his smart phone. Ian's colleague takes the seat immediately behind him, which only slightly reduces my unease. I scan the room again. The wall opposite me is partially mirrored, making the room even more impressive looking, so I can see the faces of people even if they are facing away from me. Perot is talking to one of the network camera crews, set up on the back wall with their equipment focused on the stage.

I hear a flurry of activity and see Larry Corliss enter with a small entourage. He walks straight over to Edward Perot and they shake hands; each of their faces showing what I think is genuine pleasure in seeing the other.

This is a good time to check out who might be following Corliss into the room; I scrutinize the entrance, looking carefully at the faces moving through the security gauntlet. No bells ring. So why am I feeling increasingly uneasy?

I scan the front of the room. Snakeskin boots is still hunched over his iPhone, oblivious to the entrance of either Perot or Corliss, and Ian's henchman is sitting very still behind him.

I turn my attention back to the politicians. After a few words they separate and Perot goes over to Sam. He shakes her hand and she gives him a warm smile. He says something and she laughs. I feel a stab of jealousy as she puts her hand on his forearm. She looks stunning.

I can't look at her. I turn back toward Larry Corliss. He is scanning the room and he makes eye contact with me. Leaving one of his entourage to talk to the network guys, he smiles and walks over, followed by the other two.

"Hi Cal," he extends his hand and we shake. Although I am unsure about the wisdom of his agenda to legalize all drugs, I like the man a lot and owe him big time. He turns to his two colleagues. "Could you give us a moment, please guys." They smile and one gives me a friendly nod but I sense they are not pleased. I take a second to scan the entranceway but there are no familiar faces. I check snakeskin boots but he is still tapping away at his screen.

Larry Corliss' face has lost its politician's smile. I look into worried eyes. "What's the problem, sir?"

"First thing, Cal, why don't you call me Larry?"

It catches me by surprise. "OK... Uh, Larry." I smile but his face becomes grave.

"I need your help on something. Could I ask you to attend a meeting to discuss it?"

"Of course sir," I say, inwardly cursing the fact that it's going to keep me from my next step towards finding Ariel: a visit to Mark Traynor.

"After the debate, I'll probably have to perform for the TV cameras for a while. After that, we can meet here in the hotel in the Seymour Board Room on the second floor."

"I'll be there," I assure him trying not to show my reluctance.

"Good man." I receive a pat on the shoulder and get the full force of his charismatic smile.

His news has ramped up my feelings of unease. Maybe I'm wrong in my assumption that there would not be a second attempt on his life.

The room is almost full now with most people sitting down. I check out the faces still waiting to clear security. Nothing. I walk to the front of the room and stand beside the stage. Row by row, I check each face. Except for snakeskin boots, none of them ring any warning bells.

Then I see him and my mind goes on alert.

Walking toward the stage is a man holding three microphones. It is a face I know. I move in front of the stage in his direction. "Near the mirror. Familiar face with the microphones," I say into my sleeve.

The mountain has come to Mohammed.

I focus on the mics. They look innocent enough, except that there are already three mics on the stage. Why would he be taking three more? He is almost coming up behind Sam, who has positioned herself against the mirrored part of the wall and is taking pictures of her client. Out of the corner of my eye, I see Larry Corliss step up onto the stage. The guy with the mics is not looking at Corliss but at Sam. I keep moving and intersect his path at the corner of the stage.

"Could I look at those microphones please, Mr. Traynor?"

His face registers surprise. "How did you—"

I take the mics from his hand. They are much lighter than I expected. I find the switch on one of them and turn it on. The tap of my finger booms from the ceiling speakers. Just to be sure, I repeat the procedure with the other mics before I hand them back.

"I need to speak to you some more Mr. Traynor. Can you meet me after the debate?"

"What for?" He blinks his green and brown eyes.

"I just need to ask you some more questions."

He thinks for a beat, says, "Sure," and steps up onto the stage.

"Do you know him?" Ian's voice says through my earpiece.

I walk back toward my original position. "Yeah. Right face, wrong context," I tell him. I'm pretty sure it's the wrong context. Why would the sound guy, fired by the producer of *Canada's Littlest Beauty* show up at the debate. I'm leery of coincidence but this is almost certainly just that.

Traynor replaces the hotel mics with his own and says the obligatory, "Testing, testing" into each of them before returning to his position with the TV crews.

The debate moderator takes his position at the center microphone. "Good evening, Ladies and Gentlemen. I am happy to welcome you to…" I tune him out.

Ian and two of his men are entering the room. They close

the double doors and one takes up his post in front of them. Ian walks over and stands beside me and his other colleague stands by the TV crews who are filming the debate for their networks' late news.

I look toward snakeskin boots. He is taking photos of Larry Corliss which increases my feelings of unease.

"Excuse me guys." I turn toward the whisper. It's Alexis, who works for the hotel. "You said to let you know if I saw anyone doing anything odd."

She has Ian's and my attention.

"What did you see?" Ian asks.

She addresses her answer to me. "One of our banquet servers said he saw someone in the corridor that runs behind this room and into the kitchen; he had to ask him to leave.

"Do you have a description of this person?" Ian asks.

"Yes. He said average height, sandy hair and well dressed."

I scan the room; there are at least twenty-five people who fit the description.

"Anything else?"

"Yes. He said the man had really cool boots."

"Thanks, I really appreciate it," I say and am rewarded with a lovely smile.

Within seconds Ian and I are looming over the familiar face in the snakeskin boots. Ian's colleague, sitting behind him, also stands.

"Sit down," someone hisses.

Snakeskin looks up and smiles at us. It is one of those smiles that sits on the lips and never reaches the eyes. Although he is ringed by the three of us—and there is no doubt that the other two are hard, ex-military—he shows no sign of any concern, let alone fear.

"Would you come with us please sir?" Ian says in a tone that denies there is any question in what he has just said.

Snakeskin takes a leisurely sneer at each of us, slips his iPhone into the breast pocket of his jacket and stands.

We escort him down the aisle, through the doors and into the lobby. Without asking permission, Ian frisks him thoroughly and finds nothing out of the ordinary.

Ian says, "This is a private function I'm afraid sir." He opens the door leading out onto the street.

With the same sneer playing on his lips he walks to the door but stops half-way through. He turns. "Good night, gentlemen." He looks at me and sheer malevolence sends a chill down my spine. "See you again, Rogan."

He turns and walks off.

How the hell does he know my name?

I move to follow him but Ian's hard grip encases my bicep. "We have other priorities."

He's right. Quelling my curiosity, I return with Ian and his colleague to the ballroom.

I rack my memory. Where have I seen that face before? Nothing comes.

Then a sudden, out-of-the-blue, off-the-wall intuition.

But if I'm right, how could he possibly know my name?

21

CAL

The mood has changed. Larry Corliss has gone from ebullience at what he perceives as his victory in the debate to solemnity at this meeting.

He is seated at the head of the conference table with a can of Coors Light in front of him. I am on his right and Arnold Young and Bill Watson, Larry's campaign manager, are facing me. Bill has been waxing enthusiastically about Larry's performance in the debate. In his opinion Larry won hands down.

Arnold and I sit in silence while Ian walks round the room with a device called a nonlinear junction detector looking for electronic bugs.

It is almost a year since I have been face-to-face with Arnold. He still has his ramrod-straight bearing and eagle eye but he has aged more than the twelve months would warrant. Maybe he is thinking the same thing about me.

As much as I want to help Larry, I just want to be out of here. When the debate finished, Mark Traynor was nowhere to be found. His colleagues said he left just after the debate started. I need to track him down. And I keep thinking about the guy in the snakeskin boots. All my time on the streets and as a cop has given me an antenna for detecting drug gang members and I'm sure he's one. And he's not a street-level dealer either; although he's different physically, he reminds me of 'Blondie', the number two man in a drug gang, who nearly beat me to death.

I cannot shake the feeling that snakeskin boots is the Bookman, the drug dealer whom Stammo's runaway, Tyler Wilcox, hangs out with. I want to get out of here and talk to Stammo about it. See if his snitch can confirm the Bookman's fondness for snakeskin boots. And I need to talk to Mark Traynor. I've made some progress today but not enough and every minute counts. Who knows what could be happening to Ariel.

"All clear," Ian announces. "I'll leave you gentlemen to it." He leaves and closes the conference door behind him.

"So, Mr. Corliss." Arnold calls everybody by his surname; he has called me 'Mr. Rogan' since I was twelve. "How can we help you?"

Larry Corliss takes a deep breath. "We all know that the very last thing the drug gangs want is the legalization of drugs. Well… I guess they think I'm a threat to the *status quo*. I got an email this afternoon. It contained a threat and a promise."

"If there's a threat to you don't you think we should ask Ian to step back in?" Arnold asks.

"No, it's not that sort of threat and I want to keep the circle of people who know about this to a minimum. Bill is here because he's my campaign manager and I don't keep anything from him. Arnold, I owe it to you to let you know this. You manage the funds set up by the late Mr. Wallace to help support my campaign and you need to decide whether or not to continue that support. Cal, you are here because I need someone with police experience to act for me in this. I can't take it to the VPD or RCMP."

He's got my attention.

"Ten years ago my father was very sick. He was dying, but not quickly, and he was in a lot of pain. He refused to spend his last year in the hospital so I would go over to his house a couple of times a day to look after him. He had syrup containing morphine for control of the pain. But after a while he lost so much motor control, he would drop the syrup bottle and be unable to pick it up. The first time it happened, I got over there in the evening and he was screaming in pain. He had gone six hours without the morphine. Anyway, I took a leave of absence from work—I was in the Crown Prosecutor's office at the time—and stayed with him most of the day.

"The pain started to get more frequent and I set up a meeting with his doctor. He said Dad was likely to live another six months and there was nothing more he could do for him unless he moved into a hospice. The next morning Dad said that he didn't want to go into a hospice. He asked me to gradually increase the dosage and frequency of the morphine until he didn't wake up again. I didn't want to do it but he begged me."

He stops for a moment; locked in the memory. For the first time, I notice the muted ticking of a clock on the wall.

He shakes his head as if to clear away the thoughts. "Anyway, I did as he asked. Two weeks later he was dead."

The story makes me think of Sam. At some point her MS will get so bad that she won't be able to function any more. The thought of it sends a worm of dread slithering through my intestines. Knowing Sam, she would likely ask me to help her out of her misery.

I'd want to be there for her but I don't know if I'd actually be able do it.

Larry's voice brings me back. "The email I got this morning said the sender had proof that I'd killed my father and that it would be released to the press if I didn't withdraw my candidacy."

Bill Watson is the first to react. "Who sent the email?"

"It was sent from an anonymous email service."

"Is there any way to trace it back to the sender?" Bill asks.

"I don't think so."

An idea forms in my head. "Do you still have the email, sir?"

"Yes. And it's Larry, not sir." I smile and I see Arnold frown.

"Forward it to me. I know someone who may be able to track down where it was sent from." I slide my business card across the conference table. "Assuming it was a drug gang who sent it, how did they find out? Who else knows about the circumstances of your father's death?"

"Good question. I think Dad's doctor knew, or at least guessed, but because he's a Roman Catholic, I never discussed it with him. My then-wife knew. Also, I told my younger sister and she hit the roof. She said I'd done it to get my hands on the inheritance so that I could finance my first run for Mayor."

"Can you give me names and contact information for them? If one of them leaked the information, I want to know which one and to whom they leaked it."

He nods.

We lapse into silence until Arnold breaks it.

"You said you received a threat and a promise," he says. "What was the promise?"

"The email said if I withdrew, I would receive a quarter of a million bucks 'for my trouble.'"

"That's a lot of money," Bill says.

"Not to a drug gang," Arnold counters. "Among some contacts I have in the US government, it's well known that there are as many as a half a dozen Congressmen who are on the payroll of the drug gangs to the tune of a million bucks a year each; and maybe a couple of Senators too. Their job is to ensure that US legislation stays in lockstep with the needs of the drug cartels. They make sure any legislation that even smells of legalization of drugs never gets near the statute books. A one-off payment of two hundred and fifty grand is penny-ante change to the gangs for keeping prices high and profits huge."

Larry is nodding his agreement.

A thought comes to me. "What if it's not a drug gang. What if your opponent, or someone in his camp, knew about your Dad's death and was trying to get you to withdraw."

"Long shot, Cal," Larry says. "I've known Ed Perot for quite a while and I don't think he's the type to do anything like that." I am not too sure about that. Perot seems like a nice guy but he is a politician after all and I still have my cop's natural aversion to the breed.

"Even if he did make the threat, he hasn't got the money to offer me two hundred and fifty grand to withdraw," he adds.

"Maybe, but what about one of his supporters… Dave Bradbury for example." I remember my visit to Bentley and Bradbury, Merchant Bancorp. The artwork on the office walls would pay my rent for a decade.

Arnold snorts. "David Bradbury doesn't have two pennies to rub together. We did some work for his late father-in-law's firm. The old man put a lot of money into Bradbury's firm but unfortunately he has zero talent for finance. He's made a series of spectacularly bad investments and is on the point of bankruptcy."

I think over my interview with Bradbury. When I asked him whether he had received a ransom demand, I felt something was wrong. Was it the fact that if he did receive a substantial ransom demand, he wouldn't be able to pay it?

Or what if he already has…?

A very uneasy feeling is stirring in my gut.

Larry's voice cuts into my thoughts. "Is there anything we can do gentlemen or is my run at federal politics at an end?"

There is a long silence. I think about Larry's predicament.

Either he is exposed, at the best case, for assisted suicide or, at the worst case, for manslaughter, *or* he takes the offer of the bribe.

"Why not go public with the email," I suggest. "Deny the details and blame the drug gangs for trying to silence you."

I can see Bill Watson, the campaign manager, weighing the options. "It might work," he says.

"It wouldn't." Arnold's tone is adamant. "They are not making empty threats. You can bet they have someone willing to give evidence that you killed your father. Your career would be dead and you *could* end up in jail."

"You're right," says Larry. "Maybe I should withdraw but refuse to take the bribe."

"Definitely not."

All eyes turn to Arnold. A small smile is playing on his lips. Arnold's smiles are always small.

"If we are willing to spend a little money for Mr. Rogan's services, I think we should try and turn the tables on them," he says.

In the silence, I am as confused as everyone else at the table.

22

CAL

I press all the door buzzers except one. Then wait... Suddenly a whole bunch of voices are questioning. "Hello." "Who is this? Don't you know it's almost midnight?" "Is that you Fred?" But one person figures they know who has pressed his door bell. The lock on the front door buzzes. I push it open and walk in.

The lobby smells of mold. I don't care. This is where I get to make a big move forward on Ariel's case.

According to his personnel record, given to me by Thomas Radcliffe, Mark Traynor is in apartment 505.

The elevator is old, smelly and slow.

Ellie's identification this afternoon of Sherri Oliver as the phony cop at St. Cecelia's has changed everything. The address in her personnel file was non-existent but I have this feeling in my gut that Mark Traynor might know where I can track her down. In addition to playing the female police officer, she is also the voice of Justin and deep into the kidnapping of Ariel Bradbury.

If Mark Traynor can get me a location for Sherri Oliver, this case will likely be solved. Ariel may be traumatized but she'll be home and safe.

As the elevator stops at the fifth floor, I stifle a yawn. It's been a long day.

I step out on to the stained carpet.

I wonder why Traynor lives in a place like this. He must make good money in the movie business. Maybe he's going to use the 'severance pay' he extorted from Radcliffe to get a better place to live.

Apartment 505 is directly opposite the elevator.

I didn't ring his buzzer downstairs because I don't want him to blow me off. For the same reason, I knock loudly and say "Fortis BC. Checking for a gas leak."

No response.

I put my ear to the door. I hear what sounds like a voice on the radio. Maybe a sportscast.

I knock again.

"Did you say there's a gas leak?"

The lady from 504 looks like she's at least a hundred years old.

"No ma'am. You must have misheard me. There's nothing to worry about." I say it quietly. I don't want Traynor to hear my denial.

"What did you say?"

"I said there's nothing for you to worry about. The problem is in Mr. Traynor's apartment."

She looks at me for a moment.

"Why didn't you say so before."

She turns and slams the door behind her.

I knock harder on Traynor's door.

Nothing.

The lock on the door is one of those cheap locks where the keyhole is in the door knob. No problem.

I turn the knob.

Open sesame. Easier than I thought.

The apartment smells of pizza. I close the door behind me and turn the little gizmo that locks it.

I'm in a tiny hallway. Bathroom to the left, closet to the right. There are no pictures or photos on the walls.

"Mark?"

Nothing.

"Mark. Are you home?" A little louder.

I know I shouldn't be doing this but I'm going to anyway.

I walk ahead into the living room. It's sparsely furnished but with a big screen TV showing hockey. A replay of the LA Kings getting stomped by the Canucks. He's not going to be gone long. On the opposite side of the room is an Apple MacBook. I touch the mousepad and the screen comes to life. No password. Good. I click the Spotlight icon and type Sherri Oliver.

The elevator door screeches open.

Crap.

Two quick steps to the hallway, step into the bathroom and push the door almost closed. If he comes in and doesn't need to pee, I'll be in a good position to take him. The bathroom smells of mildew. As so often happens, the smell triggers a memory, this one is of the many apartments I lived in as a kid.

Someone knocks on the door.

Pause.

Knock-knock.

Pause.

Knock-knock-knock.

"Mark?"

A woman's voice.

Silence.

I have a wild thought that it might be Sherri Oliver. Maybe I should open the door. No wait, there's a peephole.

As I step out of the bathroom, she tries the door. Thank goodness I thought to lock it.

Two steps take me to the peephole.

She's facing the elevator, her back to me, but she has the ponytail. It *is* her. Now she's going to be in for a big surprise.

The elevator door squeals open again.

I snatch open the apartment door.

She is stepping into the elevator.

"Sherri." I take a step towards her.

She turns. Scared look. "Who the hell are you?" she asks.

She's kind of cute and wholesome looking but she's not Sherri Oliver.

My mind revs. I take a step back.

"I work with Mark." It's the only thing I can think to say. "I needed to pick something up from him but he's not home."

"So how did you get in?" Very suspicious.

"The door was unlocked, so I just let myself in. Thought I'd wait inside."

I don't know if she's buying it.

"OK." She is backing into the elevator, her suspicion now laced with fear.

"Is there a message I can give Mark?" I ask.

"Uh, yes. OK." She's nervous. "Tell him Natalie was here. Tell him I'll call him."

As the elevator door starts to screech closed, I see her reach for the button to take her down.

My guess is she's Mark's girlfriend. She expected him to be here. That, combined with the TV being on, means he's almost certainly going to be back at any moment. Maybe they'll meet in the lobby. I look down the hallway. At the far end is the exit to the stairwell. Good sense demands I hightail it out of here but... curiosity triumphs over good sense.

I go back into the apartment. I go back to the Mac. I need to find any reference to Sherri Oliver.

I hear a ring tone. It's the same as Stammo's and it's coming from what I assume is the bedroom. Natalie calling to tell Mark about the stranger in his apartment? If his cell is in his bedroom, then so is he. Maybe he's a heavy sleeper.

I'm holding my breath. Waiting for the sound of his voice. It doesn't come.

The ringing stops. How sound asleep is he?

A cold finger strokes my spine. Juliet's nurse says, *Marry, and amen, how sound is she asleep!* just before she discovers…

Three strides take me to the bedroom door. I yank it open.

Three eyes stare at me. One is greenish, one is brown and the third one, drilled into the center of his forehead, is black and red-rimmed.

My hopes of saving Ariel before morning shatter into tiny pieces. Where do I go from here?

23

CAL

THURSDAY

Steve has given me the info I needed from Forensics and I feel a twinge of guilt for not reciprocating, especially seeing as he's letting me watch the interrogation through the two-way glass. I'm pretty sure Thomas Radcliffe is guilty of killing Mark Traynor to keep his dirty little secret and I'm equally sure that Steve will be able to break him. But I'm also almost certain that he is not responsible for kidnapping Ariel Bradbury and I can get Steve to test this theory.

After I found the body, I spent some time on Traynor's computer before the police arrived. I checked files, email, contact, calendar and social media sites for a reference to Sherri Oliver but could find nothing; maybe VPD forensics will unearth something. Only one thing caught my eye, an entry in his calendar, a meeting for tomorrow evening at seven o'clock. There was no name. Just a line of dollar signs followed by the words 'The Lift.'

The Lift is a high-end bar and restaurant in Coal Harbour, way beyond the means of Mark Traynor. My guess is that he thought he was going to meet Thomas Radcliffe there to get his 'severance pay.' We'll see.

In contrast to his very dapper lawyer, Radcliffe looks as worn out as I am. Steve had him arrested in the early hours of the morning on child pornography and voyeurism offenses. With the overwhelming weight of evidence garnered from a search of his office yesterday evening, Radcliffe is screwed. Satisfying, but I am impatient for him to get onto what interests me.

Steve has finished questioning him about the movies.

Time for the switch.

Fighting off the tiredness that losing a night of sleep bestows on me, I focus all my attention on Radcliffe. He's sitting at a table facing the two-way mirror and I have a ring-side seat.

"Where were you last night between eight and eleven PM?" Steve asks.

Before Radcliffe can answer, his lawyer interjects, "How is that relevant to the charges?"

"It's not," Steve says smoothly. "There's something else we need to ask your client about."

No reaction from Radcliffe.

"What specifically is that?" the lawyer asks.

"It's about Mark Traynor, a former employee of your client."

That gets a reaction. Radcliffe's pupils dilate. His lawyer's eyes narrow.

"What ab—?"

"Don't say anything, Thomas." The lawyer's eyes drill into Steve's, "What is this about Sergeant Waters?"

"Mr. Radcliffe, did you kill Mark Traynor yesterday?"

"Mark's dead?" He seems genuinely surprised.

"Don't say *anything* more, Thomas."

Steve barrels on. "Did you kill him?"

"Sergeant Waters!"

"Why would I kill Mark?" Radcliffe ignores his lawyer's instructions. He looks terrified.

"To stop him ratting you out about your kiddy-porn movies."

"I wouldn't kill—"

"Thomas, that's enough!" The lawyer's voice is a shout. He sounds like an angry parent. "Sergeant Waters, are you accusing my client of murder?"

"Not yet. I'm just trying to eliminate him from our inquiries."

"May we have a moment Sergeant?"

Steve nods and leaves the interview room. He enters the viewing room, turns off the speaker and taps on the glass. Radcliffe and his lawyer go into a huddle.

I use the break in the action. "Steve, when you go back in, ask him about firing Sherri Oliver. She's the key to Ariel's kidnapping. She was posing as the cop at the school on the day Ariel disappeared. She poses as a boy named Justin. When she gets a girl who seems like a good target, she gets a cell phone to them by leaving it in their garden. She gave one to Ellie."

"Ellie? She tried to groom your Ellie?"

I nod. "She even talked to her. When Ellie told me she had spoken to 'Justin,' I wondered if the kidnapper was using another kid, a boy, to talk to the targets. But when I was talking to Ellie about it, I heard Bart Simpson's voice on the TV. Bart's voice is done by a woman. I realized that Sherri could be Justin's voice.

"There's one of two possibilities. One is that Radcliffe is the kidnapper and Sherri Oliver is his accomplice but if that were the case, why would he have volunteered her name to me when I asked him if he had recently fired any employees. It doesn't make sense."

Steve thinks for a second and nods his head. He's not happy; he liked Radcliffe for the kidnapping.

"Radcliffe told me he found her going through some files

on his computer. Find out what files. There may be a clue to finding her."

There is a knock on the glass behind me. Radcliffe's lawyer is signaling for Steve to come back into the interview room. Steve turns the speaker back on and leaves the viewing room.

He re-enters the interview room.

"Thomas," says the lawyer, "please tell Sergeant Waters what you were doing yesterday evening."

"I was in a dinner meeting with investors from eight until close to midnight. You can check with my secretary, she was there the whole time. She can give you the names of the people I met with if you want to talk to them too."

Steve nods. "Give me the name, address and phone number of your secretary please."

Radcliffe complies and Steve casually scribbles down the details.

While he is still writing, Steve asks, "Did you have an appointment with Mr. Traynor tomorrow night at seven at The Lift restaurant?"

"No. Why would I?"

Crap. So who was Traynor going to meet? Maybe no one. Most likely Radcliffe told Traynor he'd meet him there in order to make him think he was actually going to get his 'severance pay.'

Steve ignores his question and does another switch.

"You told Cal Rogan that you fired Sherri Oliver because she was snooping in some files on your computer. What files were they, Mr. Radcliffe?"

It gets a reaction: puzzlement.

Radcliffe rubs his nose. "When I walked in on her, she had a number of files open. Files on the families of the kids on my show. I don't remember which ones."

"Any other files?"

Radcliffe slowly shakes his head but I recognize the look

on his face. He wants to be seen to be cooperating. Maybe the next thing he says will be what he thinks Steve wants to hear.

"Yeah... I remember... It wasn't a file, but she also had a window open to BC Ferries' website."

Interesting. The internet café Sherri used to communicate with the girls she has been grooming is on Salt Spring Island and, unless you have a boat or a plane, the only way to get there is by ferry.

"Do you remember which route she was looking at?"

"Yeah, it was Tsawwassen to Pender Island."

Not Salt Spring. For some reason the name of Pender Island throws up a red flag but I don't remember the context. It's something recent, but what? I must be getting old or maybe it's just the tiredness. I haven't slept for twenty-six hours and I may not sleep until I find Ariel.

I listen to Steve interrogating Thomas Radcliffe about Mark Traynor's murder but I'm only listening with half an ear.

When Steve switches to questions about Ariel's disappearance, I get up and leave. I need to check in with the Forensics guys and then find out if Stammo has come through for me again.

24

ARIEL

They let me play in the garden yesterday, it was nice but I still cried 'cos I miss Mommy and Daddy so much. *And* I wanted to see the dogs. They bark at night. But they wouldn't let me.

I've been here soooo long now. I wonder if I'll *ever* see Mommy and Daddy again. They've given me lots of toys to play with but I just want to go home.

That click! It's the key to the door. The woman who doesn't speak English. But it's not. It's that policewoman. She's not in uniform but she might... "Are you here to take me back to Mommy and Daddy?"

She smiles. "Not today but I do have some good news for you."

I run over to her. "What is it?"

"Mommy and Daddy are getting better and they will be out of the hospital soon, so you will be going home to see them very soon."

I can't stop myself from jumping up and down. "When? When? When?"

"Very soon," she says. "And do you know what? Mommy

says she really wants to see you dance for her, so she asked me to teach you some new dances. Would you like that?"

"Yes."

"And the quicker you learn the sooner you'll be seeing them."

"OK. Teach me."

"First you need to put on your costume, the red one with the cute little skirt."

"Does it have to be that one?" That was the one I was wearing when that man came to see me. He looked at me like... I dunno but it was yucky.

"Yes, sweetie, it does." She smiles but she looks a little sad.

25

CAL

Forensics said that the phone that Sherri Oliver used to call Ellie is a burner. She used it from Salt Spring, then turned it off and unfortunately, as of nine this morning, it hasn't been turned on again. Anyway, when it is, they said they'd ask Steve to call me."

Stammo grunts. "So you're thinking we're gonna see Sherri Oliver on the video my RCMP buddy emailed from Salt Spring."

"Yep."

"Well let's see. It's from last week when Ariel was on Facebook talking to 'Justin.'"

He has already queued up the tape. He hits play.

"The resolution's not great, it was from a bank machine opposite the cafe."

As we watch, a bunch of kids looking like students come out of the cafe and an elderly person walks in. Then the entrance to the cafe is blocked by a large man using the ATM. "Hurry up," Stammo tells him to no avail. He takes his time making his transaction. He leans forward to squint at the ATM's screen and we can't even see the sidewalk on either side of the cafe entrance. "Come on!" Stammo yells at him. After what seems an age he finishes his business and wanders off. Just as he does so, I catch a glimpse of the back of a girl in a ponytail going into the cafe.

"That could be her," I say and note the video's timecode. 2:57:30 PM. Just as I thought.

"You told Steve about her didn't you?" Stammo asks, ever suspicious.

"Yeah, of course."

"Good 'cos—"

"Pause it!" I yell. He does.

"What is it?"

I stare at the screen in horror. "Can you magnify that guy." I can see my finger trembling as I point. Stammo zooms in. The man is leaning against the wall just to the right of the cafe's front window. He looks like he's standing guard. Watching out for something.

My blood runs cold.

"I know that ugly great face," Stammo breathes. "Who the fuck is he, Rogan?"

"I don't know. But I've seen him before somewhere, I'm sure of it. And it doesn't feel good to me."

"What's he doing there?"

"Heck if I know, run the video."

We watch people walking past the cafe. The man seems to study each one intently as if he's looking for someone.

We wait, watching for forty-five minutes.

Then Sherri Oliver walks out of the cafe. Even with the video quality, I can tell it's her. She turns to our left and walks out of frame down the sidewalk.

A second passes, then another and then another. The man looks left and right, eases himself off the wall and follows her.

"What the—"

"Nick. I gotta go. I promised Arnold that I'd do some

things for him. I'll talk to you later. Just don't talk to anyone about what we've just seen." Even as I speak, I'm up and on my way to the door.

"Just wait a goddamn minute, Rogan—"

His voice is cut off as the door shuts behind me.

26

STAMMO

I don't feel as vulnerable as I did on Monday. I've got a blanket across my knees covering my dear old Glock 17. I'm in my wheelchair, on the edge of the tiny paved triangle known as Pigeon Park, a couple of doors away from the entrance to the flophouse. I'm surrounded by the usual trash. There's a young guy injecting himself with heroin, a bone-skinny crack-whore talking to her pimp and the usual gathering of drunks getting sloppier and louder by the minute. I'll never figure out how Rogan got to be part of this scene. He's explained it to me but I still don't get it.

I look down the street and see a face I know. It's not a happy memory. I swivel my chair away from him. Please God he hasn't seen my face; I don't want to deal with the aggravation right now.

"Hello Nicky boy." I'm out of luck. I swivel back. He towers above me, straggly hair, fat belly, tattoos. "Good to hear about your accident." He sneers. "Helps to make up for what you put me through."

"Yeah. How'd you enjoy your vacation in Millhaven, Carl?" I inch my hand under the blanket.

The name of Canada's toughest prison brings a look to his

face that makes me wish I'd kept my big mouth shut. Carl's big, ugly and mean but Millhaven is full of criminals that make him look like Mother Teresa. I'm betting his stay was not a happy one.

He leans forward and grabs the front of my jacket. I can feel his breath. Smells like something died in there. "Listen you little motherfucker," he rasps. "You ain't a cop no more so I'm going to teach you a little lesson."

His face is so close to mine that he doesn't see my hand slip under the blanket and close around the grip.

As I pull out the Glock, the front sight snags on the blanket and he sees the movement.

He's fast.

His free hand snakes down and locks over the barrel, forcing it back down between my legs.

He lets go of my shirt and I see his hand bunch into a fist. He signals the punch, big time, but in my chair there's nothing I can do to avoid it.

Shit. What am I doing out here on the streets? This is gonna hurt.

"Carl!" The voice is not loud but there is a tone of command in it.

Carl looks at the speaker who's standing behind me. There's a look on his face. Not fear exactly, more respect.

He drops his fist and lets go of the Glock. The temptation to put a bullet in his knee is big but it's not the best idea I've ever had.

I swivel the chair to look at the newcomer and I don't know which of us is more surprised.

"Tyler."

He doesn't respond to me.

"Wait for me inside," he says.

Carl nods. He looks down at me and smiles—it's not a pretty sight—then turns around, walks along the sidewalk and goes into the flophouse.

"What are you doing here, Mr. Stammo?" Suddenly the man who just gave orders to a great hulking thug is a young kid again.

This may be my only chance to talk him around. "More to the point Tyler is what are you doing here? Your Dad and Mom are worried sick about you."

"Did he ask you to track me down?" He sighs. "Yes of course he did." He looks around him. "Listen, Mr. Stammo. There's no way I'm going back. My Dad wants me to work in a factory for Chris'sakes."

"I understand that," I say. "Once I moved out here, *I* never wanted to go back east. But the people you're mixed up with are a bad crowd. I don't know much about this Bookman character you're hanging out with but he's gonna get you into a lot of trouble."

"There's a lot of stuff you don't know, Mr. Stammo. I can't just leave like that, even if I wanted to. Which I don't."

It doesn't ring true. I've got to find a way.

"Listen—"

He cuts me off quickly. "Tell Dad and Mom I'm OK and not to worry." He turns away from me. "Just leave it alone Mr. Stammo. For your own good."

The words sound threatening but somehow… I dunno.

Tyler follows the path of Carl into the so-called hotel.

There's no way they are going to let me through that door but there *is* one thing I can do. I look around and see it: a blue Shelby GT350.

I'm going to track down this Bookman character and find out what hold he's got over Tyler. I can't let him get in any deeper.

27

CAL

The loud noise is somehow soothing. Being forced to sit here has given me time to think. I'm pretty sure that the man stationed outside the cafe was a criminal of some sort. If Stammo is still speaking to me when I get back, I'll get him to send a copy of the video screenshot to his buddies in the VPD who deal with sex crimes; see if he's on their radar. The more I think it all over, the more uneasy I become.

Then out of the blue, I think of Immanuel Kant. The philosopher who impressed me most at college. One of the pillars of his wisdom was truthfulness. He posed an interesting dilemma: If you had an innocent man hiding in your house and a murderer came to your door and asked you if the man was there, would it be moral to lie and say no? Kant's view was that you should not lie even in that dire circumstance. He allowed that you could be evasive, but not lie directly.

It's only just afternoon and I've lied to both Steve and Stammo. In fact, it's not just today. I have told a fair bunch of lies and perpetrated a fair number of evasions since I started on Ariel's case. And it's pressing heavily on my conscience.

My desire to find her first is born out of the need to beat the Department to the punch. If I were to die right now, the information in my head would be lost, to the detriment of solving the case. I should—

My phone rings. It's Steve. I'm betting that Stammo has told him about the tape and about Sherri Oliver. I should talk to him myself and tell him the other things I know or suspect. I look at the phone… and press the red button. I'll come clean with Steve tomorrow. I see Kant look at me and shake his head.

As if to annoy me, the phone rings again. It's Arnold. I feel a touch of guilt that I haven't even thought about Larry Corliss' problem. I tap my earpiece.

"Hi Arnold." I don't add 'what's new?' or 'how can I help you?'. Arnold doesn't do small talk.

I strain to hear him over the background noise. *"Our plan seems to be working. Larry Corliss contacted the blackmailer via the anonymous email account, accepted the bribe and demanded that it be in cash. They told him they'd be in touch. I may be needing your assistance in surveillance on short notice. Be at my office at eight-thirty tomorrow."* It's not a request.

Before I can ask one of the questions bubbling to the surface, he hangs up.

I resist the temptation to call him back; I need to deal with what's important right now.

The background noise changes; it drops in pitch. I look out the window at the waters of Long Harbour and hope that I don't die when the plane lands on them.

———

THE TINY TOWN of Ganges on Salt Spring Island has more than its fair share of coffee shops. I am sitting in one, drinking what is probably the best Americano I've ever tasted, and looking out the window at the coffee shop opposite. It's the internet cafe which Sherri Oliver uses to pose as Justin. Stammo was as mad as hell when I called but agreed to do as I ask. I'll be the object of a tongue-lashing when I get back to the office.

It's just after three and I've been watching people come and go for about half an hour. The streets are busy for a cold afternoon in March. Then I see her, ponytail pushed through the back of her LA Dodgers baseball cap, dressed in high-end jeans tucked into higher-end boots. I only have the skeleton of a plan but I'm going to give it the good old college try. I can't see any sign of the bodyguard she had on the video. I scan the faces moving in the same direction as her and no one looks out of place: an old couple, a young kid, some teenagers. No one who looks even vaguely like a bodyguard. Maybe fortune smiles on the semi-prepared.

I send a quick text, leave the warmth of my cafe and cross the cold street. Another scan in each direction reveals no suspicious faces. I walk into the internet cafe and a bell jangles above my head. It seems like an anachronism in the cafe's hi-tech style. I stand behind Sherri at the counter.

"The usual?" The teenager behind the counter is clearly smitten.

"Thanks Dale and I only need one hour today."

He takes her money and hands her a slip of paper. "Number four. I know it's your fav. I'll bring you your latte."

By the look on his face, she gave him a big smile as she dropped her change into the tip jar. She walks over to the computers and takes a seat at the one with a big #4 sign clipped to the monitor. I can see why it's her favorite. The chair has its back to the wall so that no one can sit behind her.

I order an Americano but Dale the Barista doesn't offer to bring it to me. There is a counter with high stools that faces out through the window. I take a seat and text again then look out the window, facing away from her. I definitely don't want her—or anyone else observing me as I observe her—to spot me as a tail. *Ping*. It's a text back from Stammo. *Justin messaging me.* Great. Stammo is logged into Ellie's Instagram account.

I need to push down the anger that is building up in me. She thinks she's grooming my daughter. The desire to turn around and look at her is almost overwhelming. The desire to go over and strangle her is even greater. But I must keep the objective in mind. We need to find out where she goes because maybe that's where we'll find Ariel and because maybe when we do find her she'll be alive. I'm just praying that Stammo hasn't told his RCMP buddy over here. The last thing I want is Sherri Oliver spooked by a uniform.

I suggested a f2f. "Good" I text back. No response. I turn around to see if the barista has made my Americano. He is walking over to Sherri with a large latte in his hand and a larger grin on his face. I so want to follow him with my eyes and look at her, look at the face of the monster who abducted Ariel and probably that girl from Coquitlam and probably others and who wants to do the same to my Ellie. But I don't. I turn back to the window.

There are people walking by. Out of habit, I scan the faces looking for anyone who might trigger a memory or even an uncomfortable feeling. Nothing. Just normal people going about their business. Most likely all locals. The tourist season is a couple of months away. A pretty girl walks by. She's holding hands with a biker; he's wearing a bandana, leathers, chains and boots and sporting a beard cut just right. But he doesn't have the look.

She turned down f2f for next week. Said maybe week after. "Good" I text again. And it is good. If she's not ready to snare Ellie, Ariel is probably still alive.

"Quad-shot Americano." yells Dale. I get up from my seat and walk over to retrieve it. There is a lull in the action and he is looking at her like I used to look at Sam. Another pang.

"Your girlfriend?" I ask quietly.

"I wish," he sighs.

"You should ask her out."

He unconsciously shakes his head. "I want to but, you know…" I do. I don't want to be unkind to him but she's a bit out of his league. "Anyway, she's not from around here."

Damn!

"Where's she from?"

"Dunno." The tingle stops.

"She comes from one of the other islands."

I nod. "That's tough."

"She comes here by boat."

He's giving me information and I don't want to freak him out by being too inquisitive, so I just say "Uh-huh."

"Yeah." He gives me a quirky grin. Seems like a nice kid. "Big fancy boat. I followed her one time—" He stops short and blushes. "I wasn't stalking her or nothing, I just…"

Ping. I glance at my phone. *"Says she's gtg."*

"Don't worry. If I was twenty years younger I'd have done the same thing." I give him a big smile. "She must have money. Why does she come here to use your computers? She must have one of her own."

"I dunno, I'm just glad she does."

The bell over the door rings merrily and three teenagers come in, all wearing high-end clothes. Dale seems to know them and I know our conversation is over. I got a lot more than I expected.

If she comes here by boat, it probably ties up at the government dock a couple of hundred yards down the street. As I walk back to the counter by the window, I risk a glance at her. She is bent over the keyboard typing. I wonder if there is another eight- year-old girl whom she is putting into her evil inventory.

I look out the window again and sip the Americano. Not nearly as good as the one across the road. Maybe rather than follow her, where I might get spotted by any bodyguard she may have, I should leave ahead of her and make my way to the government dock. Then I look across the road and see the perfect place.

Without a glance in her direction, I leave the cafe and the coffee, cross the road and walk into the local bookstore. I stroll over to the closest shelf and select a book at random. I stand where I can look out the window and watch the door of the internet cafe while pretending to be interested in *Flower Arranging for the Novice.* Apart from the clerk and me, the shop is empty.

Minutes pass and I learn the basics of flower arranging. It's more interesting than I thought. For example, I didn't know that—

"It's good isn't it?" She's about sixteen and she could be the sister of Dale the barista.

"Yes. I didn't know there was so much to it."

"There's actually another one here that you might be interested in." She pulls a bigger, more opulent-looking book off the shelf. Trying to up-sell me. She opens it and starts to wax enthusiastic about the merits of the more expensive item. I divide my attention between watching the door across the street and pretending to be interested in her patter. She helps pass the time. It's pleasant.

Then as always happens on stakeouts, the action starts fast. A man walks along the street and I know him. Well, not actually know him but know the type. He's the muscle. The type that every criminal organization needs. It's not the guy from the bank machine's video but it might as well be. It's not just his build, or his clothes or even the look on his face, but his very being screams out the word thug. I'm completely focused on him.

"Is it for you or is it a gift?"

"A gift," I say absently.

He walks into the internet cafe and in my mind I hear the

chime of the bell above the door. Sherri and muscleman. My heart pounds, I think I know what this means.

"Would you like me to wrap it for you?"

"That would be great."

I strain to look through the window but I really can't see anything other than vague movement. I hear the rustle of paper behind me. I might as well buy it. It will give me the look of a person who belongs in the scene when I start trailing her.

An elderly couple of men appear from stage right and start to enter the cafe. They hold back as Sherri exits and, as suspected, she is followed by the muscle. I need to move now.

"I'll come back for it in five minutes," I say.

"Just hang on it's almost done." But I'm already halfway out the door. I turn away from my quarries and walk along my side of the street toward the park near the ramp to the government dock. As I reach the end of the street, I turn and look both ways while crossing. They are about fifty feet behind me; it's a good surveillance technique to be in front of your subjects for a while. I walk into the park and immediately see my prop. Big, blonde and beautiful. Stammo would hate her. I walk over to her and smile, and she responds with a gentle wagging of her tail. I crouch down and let her smell my hand then stroke her head and scratch that spot behind the ear that nearly every dog loves.

"Well, you're a lovely girl aren't you?" I say, glad that dogs aren't sensitive to the patronizing way we talk to them. But it's not for her benefit.

I hear rather than see Sherri and the muscle pass behind me. I give them some time then, with a final scratch behind the ear straighten up and follow them. My goal is clear. Get the name and registration of the boat that is going to whisk Sherri and her muscle away. I pick up a discarded newspaper from a park bench as I pass and stuff it under my arm. I'm just

ROBERT P. FRENCH

another citizen out for a stroll. As they approach the ramp down to the dock, I notice a second man standing there. I recognize him immediately. He's the man from the bank machine video. He looks toward me and I am close enough to see a look of shock in his eyes. He says something to Sherri and her escort and the latter looks back at me as the former trots briskly down the ramp. There is recognition in his eyes too.

How the heck do *they* know *me*? I'm pretty sure I've never seen either of them before. As I approach the ramp the guy from the video blocks my path. Behind him my quarries are running down the dock.

Still playing the part of a citizen out for a stroll, I say, "Excuse me," and start to squeeze past him. Unexpectedly, he moves back and as my momentum carries me forward, he trips me up. Suckered. My head explodes in a galaxy of stars.

Disorientation

Has time passed?

Someone is helping me to my feet. "Are you OK mate?" Australian. I focus on him. He's concerned. "I saw it all," he says. "That bastard tripped you up and kicked you in the head."

I stand up straight and look down at the dock. It's empty. "Where did he go?" I ask.

"Ran down and got into that ruddy great boat." I follow his pointing finger and see a long sleek boat disappearing down Long Harbour. It's way too far off to get any details.

I've screwed it up royally. Stammo was right and he's going to be pissed. Now that they know I'm on to them, Sherri is never coming back to use the internet cafe. Tomorrow will be one week from Ariel's disappearance and I've screwed up our best lead. And ruined the hopes of Dave the barista.

28

CAL

FRIDAY

This time a maid answers the door. I am expected and am ushered into Rebecca Bradbury's study.

Like my last visit here, tea is poured even though it won't be consumed. Not by me anyway.

Since my visit to Salt Spring Island, I have wondered how I am going to break this to Rebecca. Break it to her that this is not just some kidnapping. Sherri Oliver had two thugs helping her; maybe there are more. This is a gang operation. But the full import of this is that they are probably taking kids and selling them into some sort of slavery. Ariel could be anywhere in the world. Another of the estimated ninety million slaves sold worldwide.

"Please sit down Mr. Rogan."

I obey. She stands.

"An update please." Imperious.

As gently as I can I say, "I think you should sit down Mrs. Bradbury."

Her face goes white and she takes a faltering step to the nearest chair.

When she is seated, I tell her that we know who abducted

her daughter and I tell her my suspicions about the possibility of a slave trading gang.

As I tell her, her eyes are darting around the room as if looking for a way out. Not out of the room but out of the obvious conclusion of my story.

"But maybe I'll get a ransom demand. Maybe they kidnap for ransom."

Just to check I ask, "Have you received a ransom demand?" Like her I want it to be a kidnap for ransom. What I believe to be the truth is unthinkable.

"No. No, I would tell you if I had, I promise you."

"Have you spoken to your husband; has he received a demand?"

"I haven't, so I don't know."

I check my watch, I don't want to be late for my eight-thirty AM meeting with Arnold. Rebecca frowns. Thinking of Arnold takes me back to the debate at the Waterfront. When Dave Bradbury arrived, he didn't look like a man whose daughter had just been kidnapped. Before I think it through I ask, "Mrs. Bradbury, I—"

"Please don't call me that anymore. I am going back to my maiden name, Jones."

I'm still going to ask it. "Ms. Jones, I want you to answer this truthfully. Is Mr. Bradbury Ariel's biological father?"

Her eyes become like saucers and drill into me. The tendons in her neck stand out and all she can do is expel a strangled gasp. She is going to hit me with both barrels. Then she kind of deflates. Her voice is barely a whisper. "How could you possibly know that?"

I don't tell her it was a wild-assed guess. It makes sense: he's going broke and needs money. Why not fake the kidnapping of her daughter to squeeze money from her. Except that Ariel's been gone for a week and she hasn't received a demand yet. Maybe he's playing a waiting game, ratcheting up her anxiety level so that she'll cave when the demand comes. That's cruel, bitterly cruel. Bradbury didn't seem that depraved when I met him.

I just look at Rebecca and wait…

Finally, "Even he doesn't know."

What! How would he not know. But if he doesn't know… Surely no man could do that to his own daughter.

"Are you sure?" I ask.

She nods and bites her lower lip. And then decides. "David had left on a long business trip to South America. Our marriage was starting to deteriorate, even back then. I had an affair, it was a one-time thing and please don't ask me with whom. When David came back I was already two weeks late. I made sure that I slept with him on the night of his return but when Ariel was born I could see who her natural father was. Until now, I have never told anyone and I am trusting you Mr. Rogan to keep it completely confidential."

This is the first time I have seen her without her patrician shield. In her vulnerability she seems so much younger and somehow fragile. "I give you my word." I have said that to perpetrators, witnesses and victims before but this time I really mean it.

"Did you think he might have taken Ariel?" she asks.

"Well, I thought it might be a possibility."

"He would never do that. He loves Ariel."

But I'm not going to let it go.

"Did you know that his business is on the point of bankruptcy?"

"I do. But he knows that my trust fund is set up such that no-one can get at the capital, not even me."

We sit in silence for a while and for the first time I take the time to look around the room. It is typical old-money Shaughnessy. There is dark wood paneling that goes halfway up the walls and above that there are a bunch of family pictures, some of them very old. Among the newer pictures is one of the Bradburys with a babe in arms, probably Ariel. They are standing on a balcony and behind them is an unique-looking seascape with islands in the distance; it looks like pictures I've seen of Thailand. The shape of the islands is unusual; they look like a dragon with his head in the water. The Bradburys looked so happy then, Rebecca is laughing, Dave is looking at her adoringly. It makes me sad.

"Was there anything else Mr. Rogan?" The patrician attitude has returned.

I get up to leave. "That's a lovely photo," I say.

"Yes." She smiles wistfully. "Happier days."

She walks me to the front door and shakes my hand.

"I'm going to do everything I can to get Ariel back," I tell her. But how? I only know what my next step is going to be and have no idea what's beyond that.

I can feel the depression settling onto my shoulders. A hit of heroin would be so sweet right now.

———

TO SAY Arnold's office is austere would be like saying the Antarctic is a bit chilly in winter. Seems fitting.

The four of us are seated at a table. Larry Corliss looks like I feel—he does not want to be here; Ian Peake is sitting ramrod straight framed by the sunny window behind him he looks a little like a Norse god—a simile he would approve of; Arnold is... well, just Arnold.

"As you know Mr. Rogan, yesterday Mr. Corliss withdrew his candidacy and the press is an uproar." I nod like I know all this; fact is I haven't had time to catch up on the news and anyway I want to be out of here as fast as I can; I need to bounce my last-ditch plan for finding Ariel off Stammo.

"True to their word, the next day the blackmailers transferred a quarter of a million dollars to his account. It was transferred from an account in Switzerland. Normally this would be completely untraceable but, as you know, I have contacts there and I was able to ascertain that the account was owned by a Corporation called Razor Point Holdings. Unfortunately, *it* is incorporated in the Cayman Islands and try as I might I have been unable to find out who controls it."

I wonder what this has to do with me.

"So we need to find some other line of investigation. What do you suggest?"

I think for a bit. No one speaks.

"If we can't follow the money then we need to know who benefits from your withdrawal from the race. Because of your stance on legalizing drugs it would almost certainly be a drug gang. Only a drug gang could afford to pay you that much to stay out of politics. There are several gangs who could afford it but my bet would be that Carlos Santiago is the most likely."

Nods all around the table. Silence.

"Also your opponents benefit. Of the people left in the race for the seat, only Ed Perot has a chance. With you out the way, as the incumbent, he's a shoe-in."

Corliss objects. "Cal, Arnold disagrees with me but I've known Ed Perot for years, he's a good man. I can't imagine that he would be involved in this."

I think back to the debate between Corliss and Perot on Tuesday evening. I got a good feeling about Perot but I'm willing to play the devil's advocate here. "If Santiago is blackmailing you to stay out of the race, I'll bet he would be funding Perot's campaign through some third party. But I don't know how we might find that out."

"I might," Arnold chips in. "Let me look into that. Meanwhile, it would be good if you, Mr. Rogan, investigate Ed Perot and see if he is as squeaky clean as he seems."

Why do I feel that this request was a foregone conclusion, that I have been manipulated into taking on a project that I really don't want?

I go to object but stop myself. There's no way Arnold will let me off this hook.

29

STAMMO

I t says Siegel's on the bag he's carrying. No way Rogan, you are not going to patch this over with bagels, cream cheese and lox.

"Hey Nick."

I don't answer, just pick up the phone and dial. When Steve answers, I put him on speaker.

"Hi Steve. Rogan's here now. Let's talk." Rogan looks embarrassed. So he should.

"Hi guys."

I'm gonna take charge of this call. "First thing, Rogan's gonna give you a debrief on his trip to Salt Spring."

"Good." Steve manages to put a lot of sarcasm into that one word.

Rogan gives him the full rundown on his fuck-up. He has the good grace to apologize a couple of times too.

When he's finished, Steve says, *"You should have told me first, Cal. I could have had someone there from the RCMP detachment. We could have arrested this Sherri Oliver and at least one of her gang. One of them would have flipped on the other during interrogation. Now, we've got nothing."*

"Yeah, I know, I know. I'm sorry Steve."

"I'm sending a member over to Salts Spring to keep an eye on that cafe and look out for the boat they escaped on but it's probably a waste of time. I should charge you for the expense of sending him there." Rogan cuts me a glance and I nod. Yes, Rogan, I already gave Steve all the details of your fuck-up.

"I'm also sending a man to Pender Island. That was the direction the boat was going right?"

A puzzled look runs across Rogan's face. "I don't know, Steve," he says. "I've never really looked at a map of the Gulf Islands."

I jump in. "Well I have. If you take a boat out of Long Harbour and keep going you get to Pender Island."

"Oh," is all he can say.

"Cal, you've shown that you can't cooperate with us, so I want you to drop this case."

Shit. Steve didn't tell me that was on his mind. The Bradbury broad's a big client in terms of dollars. I gotta—

"I can't do that Steve," he says "I won't stop until I find Ariel. Dead or alive. But I promise I will keep you in the loop on everything I do."

"Yeah. Well OK." Steve knows he can't stop us investigating. *"But you'll excuse me if I don't do the same for you."* This is not going well. We need the help of the VPD if we're gonna do a job for Rebecca Bradbury, not to mention a bunch of other cases.

Steve asks Cal a few questions on the details of his Salt Spring trip and is about to hang up when Cal stops him.

"Before you go Steve, how's the case on the kiddy-porn guy Thomas Radcliffe?"

I wonder why he's interested. We know Radcliffe didn't have anything to do with Ariel's kidnapping. Maybe he's just making nice with Steve.

"Yeah, he tried to get bail but we scotched that, we've got him dead to rights on the porn charges. I've got a team investigating the murder of Mark Traynor and we may be on to something. There was

some DNA evidence that Radcliffe had been at Traynor's place. We went through Traynor's computer with a fine-tooth comb and we found a letter that looked like a blackmail letter except that it didn't mention Radcliffe or indeed any specific person. It was all a bit vague."

"OK, thanks Steve."

"Oh, Nick. I talked to the Drug Squad this morning, they're trying hard to get some info on that Bookman guy. I asked them to keep you in the loop."

When Steve hangs up there's an uneasy silence.

Rogan gets up and brings a couple of plates and knives from the kitchen then goes back for glasses. He spreads out the contents of the Siegel's bag and cracks open a couple of cans of Talisman. Boy he's really trying to win me over.

"I'm sorry Nick."

What can I say? 'So you should be?' 'Sorry doesn't cut it?' 'Don't let it happen again?'

I settle for, "OK."

As we eat, he tells me about his meeting with Rebecca Bradbury. I can't believe that her husband didn't know that the kid's not his. I've seen too many marriages in difficulty where one parent uses the kids against the other; kidnapping's a bit extreme but you never know. Plus it would require Bradbury to be mixed up with some pretty unpleasant characters.

"I've got some new work out of Arnold," he says. Normally I'd be happy but we are slammed; we've got to get ourselves an assistant. With him spending so much time on the Bradbury kid I'm doing all the work on the projects we had before. *Plus* I want him to help me on tracking down Tyler; I proved to myself last night that I can't do it alone. It still burns.

"Cal," I say. He looks at me and there's a kindness in his eyes.

"Tyler?" he asks.

"Yeah."

"Hey, that reminds me. There's something I forgot to ask you. This Bookman character, does he ever happen to wear snakeskin boots?"

"Dunno. I'll ask Eddie. Why."

"There was a guy at the Corliss debate who had the look. I just have this nagging intuition he might be the Bookman. Probably wrong."

"Not good news for Corliss if he was," I say and he just nods.

"Anyway Nick, how can I help with Tyler?" he asks.

"I saw him yesterday."

"Your voice tells me it didn't go well," he says.

"Nah. Like you suspected, he didn't want to know me. Said he was doing OK but something didn't feel right y'know. It was like… I dunno. He said he wanted to be with the gang but he also kinda said he couldn't leave even if he wanted to. He showed up in that car owned by the Bookman."

"Did you get the plate?"

"Yeah but it was registered to a company. I looked 'em up but couldn't find anything on them. No website, nothing in the Federal or Provincial company listings. It was like they didn't exist."

"Drugs for sure."

"Yeah." I can hear the despair in my own voice.

"You'll track him down, Nick. If anyone can it's—"

Even I hear the sigh that I give. Thank God I don't have to beg. I was prepared to, for sure. Instead I tell him what I need him to do. He agrees. No ifs ands or buts.

It takes a while and another couple of Talismans to work out how we're gonna divide the workload before he goes out to start his part of the investigation into Perot and follow the only lead he's got on Ariel. Then I realize, he didn't tell Steve about that. Shit.

30

CAL

I rony. Doing a B and E to help a cop. It's just what I'm going to do right now. I don't really want to do it but Stammo promised Steve that we'd help with the Mark Traynor murder investigation. I really resent the time but I can't follow my lead on Ariel until this afternoon anyway, so I'm going to break into Thomas Radcliffe's office this morning.

It's an older building and there are only four offices per floor. The door marked *Radcliffe Productions* and *Canada's Littlest Beauty* has a fairly old style of lock which should succumb to the lock-pick set I keep in my possession—a piece of evidence from one of the first cases I worked when I was with VPD. I may not have to use it; maybe the old plastic trick will work. I turn the door handle so that I can see if the door will move enough for me to slide my celluloid strip between it and the doorframe.

I almost fall into the reception area when the door opens fully.

Radcliffe's secretary grins at my awkward entry. It's a friendly grin. Then she remembers the last time I was here. I need to turn that around.

I give her my best smile. "To tell the truth, I was expecting the office to be closed, what with Mr. Radcliffe being in prison. I'm surprised you're still here. You must be a very loyal person."

She melts just a bit. "Yes, well…"

I give her a sympathetic smile. "I work quite closely with the police and they are going to be charging him with the murder of Mark Traynor."

There is a look of panic in her face. "No, no they can't. He was in an investor meeting for *Beauty* when that little worm was killed. I told the police." There is something else in her face too.

"You told the police that?" I ask and the look gets more intense. She's flustered. This may not be the outcome I was expecting.

Before waiting for an answer, I say, "You see, the police have DNA evidence and a blackmail note that Traynor sent to Mr. Radcliffe."

"But he didn't do it. Tom would never kill someone. I just know." Tom eh? Not Thomas or Mr. Radcliffe.

I switch tracks for a moment.

"How long have you worked for him?"

Her face morphs from fluster to something much softer. "Three years. Just before he started *Canada's Littlest Beauty*."

"You like it here?"

"Oh yes. It's so interesting and Mr. Radcliffe is a wonderful boss." I can see it in her eyes. I think I do anyway. Oh well, here goes.

"You love him don't you."

She stares at me for a moment, then nods, afraid to say it out loud. Tears are starting to spring into her eyes.

"What's your name?" I ask gently.

"Adriana."

"Listen Adriana. The evidence against Tom is pretty over-whelming. The one piece of evidence in his favor is your alibi that he was at an investor meeting at the time of the murder. The police may well be interviewing the people who were at the dinner meeting. If they find any discrepancy in your alibi for Tom, they are going to be coming here and arresting you for obstruction of justice. You could go to jail for that."

She goes from lovelorn to stricken.

"But Tom didn't do it. I know he would never kill anyone."

"But you did lie to the police didn't you."

A pause. A long pause. I let it run.

Finally, "Yes."

If I do this right, I'm going to get the truth, the whole truth.

"I think I can help you. You look like you could do with a coffee. Why don't you close the office and we'll go up the street to the Blenz."

Her sign of relief is heartfelt.

Steve wanted us to find evidence for Radcliffe's innocence in the murder of Traynor and so did I for that matter. Seems like I did the opposite.

31

SAM

I go to the door. Not limping too much, no stick. The MS is in remission. I check through the peephole and feel a twinge of sadness that some of the events of the past have made me more cautious than I would like.

Cal is standing there holding a bunch of daffodils. Even through the fish-eye lens, I can see he's as nervous as a schoolboy on a first date. Why would that be? Why is he bringing me flowers? I wish I had my camera in my hand; I'd love to catch him in this moment. Somehow through the lens I seem to see the real truth of a person. Oh, Cal. I feel a tear welling up but I blink it away, put a big smile on my face, throw open the door and say, "Hi Cal, come in."

He grins back. "Hi." He thrusts the flowers into my hand. "For you."

"Daddyyyyy!" Ellie bounces down the stairs and throws herself into his arms. As always, he spins her around, plants a big kiss on her cheek and carries her into the house.

"What are we going to do today, Daddy?" she asks.

He puts her down. "Well about that sweetie—" Oh, no.

"What? What? What?" She bounces up and down in anticipation.

Too many times Cal has cancelled his time with Ell and it's always because of some work thing. It really hurts her because she idolizes him. I'll be furious if—

"Well," he says dragging out the word. Looking guiltily at her.

"What, Daddy?"

He looks at me and sees the anger in my face. Anger for Ell and anger for me. I need tonight free.

He looks back at Ell, thinks for a moment and then smiles, "Well, Elles Bells, we are going on a trip." He does a Groucho Marx thing with his eyebrows. "We're going to take a float-plane and spend today and tonight on a place called Pender Island."

"I love it. When are we leaving?"

"Right now. We're going to explore the island and walk on the beaches and eat in restaurants and stay up late and stay at a B & B."

"A B & B!" She starts bouncing again. "A B & B, a B & B!"

She stops bouncing and turns to me. "Mommy, what's a B & B?"

Cal starts laughing and I join in, as much for relief as for humor. It feels good. Still laughing I head for the kitchen to make coffee, painfully aware that my laughter could turn to tears at any second.

———

"How's your thing with Perot going?" The question jolts me. How the hell does he know?

"What thing?" I ask. I cringe at the defensive sound of my voice.

"You know, the photos you're doing for him."

I try not to show my relief. "Oh. Yes. Good. He's very photogenic. You should check his website, they're all up there."

"What's he like?" The question seems innocent enough but with Cal you never know.

"Why?" I spot the tone in my voice again.

He looks puzzled. "Well with Larry Corliss out of the race, as the incumbent he's a shoe-in. I was wondering what sort of politician he is."

"He's a really nice guy. Very thoughtful and very smart." I better pre-empt. "He was so happy with the photos I took on Tuesday that he took Ell and me out to dinner last night."

"Wow, he must have been very impressed. Two days after you took the photos." Oh God, he's suspicious.

"It was no big deal. He'd had a business meeting planned and had the reservation but the meeting was cancelled at the last minute, so he took us." The truth. Up to a point.

"Has he been in politics long?" he asks.

Phew, good, a change of subject. "Not that long. He came straight out of business to win the federal seat eight years ago. He's a successful entrepreneur. He has, or should I say had, a food importing company. Imported a lot of stuff from Asia, mainly Thailand. He loves Thailand. Says the Thais are lovely people." I realize I'm wittering on about him but it's neutral territory. "When he talks about the natural beauty he gets almost, I don't know, poetic."

"Is he married?"

Less neutral. I just say, "Widowed."

Ell comes downstairs with her pink backpack of stuffies. "Let's go Daddy," she says effectively stopping the interrogation. Well, it felt like an interrogation.

Cal finishes his coffee and gets up.

"Let's go Elles Bells," he yells, matching her enthusiasm.

He picks her up and twirls her around.

"So I'll drop her off here tomorrow?"

"Yes." I take Ell from his arms and give her a big hug. "Have a terrific time with Dad my wonderful girl."

"I will Mommy." She hugs me again.

I put her down and they march to the front door. He opens the door and takes her hand then turns to face me. "Why don't you come with us?" he says.

"I can't," I say and part of me wishes it were not so.

"Why not?" he persists. I look at him. Why is he asking? Am I wrong about his feelings? But I can't take that chance, can I?

"I have some things I have to do."

He looks disappointed but Ellie giggles and looks at me. I smile back at her wondering if an eight year-old can keep a confidence. I gently grab her nose and give it a little shake. "Remember what we agreed," I say.

"I will," she giggles again.

"You will what?" Cal asks.

"Girl's secrets," Ellie says. I smile to cover my worry that she may break under any gentle interrogation he may give her.

"'Bye Mommy."

"'Bye sweetie. 'Bye Cal."

He gives me that quirky smile of his. "See you tomorrow."

We exchange mad waving as they head down the steps, through the front yard and into his car. After they have driven off, I close the door.

Damn you, Cal. You are being the mad, wonderful, impulsive man I used to love, all over again.

32

STAMMO

Here again. The streets of the downtown east side. I don't have my Glock with me but I'm in my van so I'm safe from any encounters I might have with pissed-off ex-cons. I've just driven the streets looking for familiar faces, faces who might know something about the Bookman and be willing to tell me. I've drawn a blank. Not even my old buddy Eddie is around.

Ever since Bob called me about Tyler, I've been thinking about Matt. I know I was a crap father but I want to see him again. And Lucy. Since the brush with death that put me in this wheelchair and this modified van, I've wanted to make amends with my kids. Maybe go and see them in Toronto. Maybe I should call my ex, except it's afternoon back east; she'll have started drinking by now. Maybe I'll call Bob later, see if he can do a bit of quid pro quo; help me track down Matt.

Maybe, maybe, maybe. Maybe I'll have a beer and go home.

I find a meter a block from the Cambie pub, put down the ramp and roll down in the chair. I put the ramp up, lock the doors and make my way to the pub. I like the Cambie. It's old style. Not like the places that are springing up everywhere, catering to the young and the wealthy. I'll just have one—

The Shelby!

It's stopped at the lights going South on Cambie. If I can just get close enough to it maybe I can talk to Tyler again. Get him to— Wait. Maybe the Bookman's driving. If I could get my eyes on him. As I get closer, I can see there's a passenger who's blocking my view of the driver. He's a man about my age, well-groomed, wearing a shirt and tie and his face is familiar. Could he be Carlos Santiago? His eyes meet mine. I definitely know him from somewhere but he shows no signs of recognition. I'm just another wheelchair person in the downtown east side. He looks away, the lights change and the Shelby accelerates away. There's no way I could get back to my van, get myself inside and follow but I gotta remember that face, something tells me it's important.

Real important.

33

CAL

I t was the best of times, it was the worst of times. The best being my time with Ellie: from the short floatplane flight in the brilliant Spring sunshine, to the exploration of one of the few beaches on the island—where we found tiny crabs and wiggly things under rocks—to this lovely moment on the deck of our B&B. The worst being that I have visited most of the marinas on the island and none of them have responded to my only clue in the search for Ariel. I showed the picture to every person in every marina but no one recognized it. Although I couldn't get the registration details of the boat that Sherri Oliver escaped in, I saw enough of it to be able to find a picture online that resembled it enough to maybe identify it. But I guess not. And no one recognized Sherri Oliver either. Maybe I'll get lucky tomorrow?

"Can we go have dinner now, Daddy?" Her happy little voice pulls me out of the down mood.

"Sure sweetie."

I swallow the last of my gin and tonic and reluctantly pull myself out of my chair. I look out over the water and am amazed once again at the beauty of the Gulf Islands and grateful that I live in Vancouver and can visit them at any time. As I take in the view, I am struck by its familiarity. I've seen this specific view before. It's unusual. It reminds me of...

Then I get it. The picture on Rebecca Bradbury's wall. The one with her and her husband and baby Ariel. The view behind them looks just like this view. The dragon with his head in the water. Except that it's wrongly oriented.

"Come *on*, Daddy, I'm hungry."

I try to remember the details of the picture. If I were further north... I look to my left. There is a wooded promontory about a mile or so away. I know I need to go there.

"OK, Elles Bells, let's go."

———

As I DRIVE I can see the promontory on my right. I've just passed one of the marinas nestled in a pleasant cove. If I take the next right it should take me where I want to go. There's the road. I turn right and accelerate, enjoying the growl of the exhaust. The area is heavily wooded and I can't see any signs of habitation. As I come to the end of the road, there is just a dirt driveway left. I take it and wind my way carefully through the trees which form a canopy over our heads. I'm glad we are in a pickup truck from the island's only rental agency; the Healy would almost certainly bottom out on the uneven surface.

"This is a funny place for a restaurant," Ellie chimes in.

"The restaurant's not here Elles, I just need to stop here for a moment."

The driveway bursts out of the trees and facing us is a beautiful house. A kind of rustic villa high up overlooking the ocean.

"Wait in the car for a moment, sweetie."

I get out of the truck. The place looks deserted. Like it hasn't been lived in for a while. Not exactly abandoned but empty. Lonely. Behind us the sun is westering and the house is completely under the shadow of the forest. I walk to the windows to the right of the door and peer in. The ground floor is open plan. It is one huge floor with wooden pillars holding the beams upon which the upper floor rests. The furniture is draped in dust covers and I can imagine that there are cobwebs forming in the corners of the ceiling.

Everything is silent.

I can see through the house to the deck at the back. I don't even have to go around the house to know that the photo on the wall of Rebecca's living room was taken from there.

I don't know what it means. But it means something.

I hear a scuffing noise behind me and I turn.

"Sweetie, I told you to—"

I'm looking into the twin barrels of a shotgun. My spine goes electric.

"What the fock dj'think yer doin'" The voice has an accent. Irish maybe or more likely Newfoundland.

I glance over at the truck. Ellie's eyes are like saucers. She has seen a gun before, when she was five. The circumstances were not optimal.

"Put that down," I tell him. "You're frightening my daughter."

The gun does not waver a millimeter.

"I said, what the fock yer doin', bye." Definitely Newfie, especially that last word.

"My name's Cal Rogan." I say it calmly and reasonably. "I am a private detective helping the Bradburys with the disappearance of their daughter. I thought while I happened to be on Pender Island, I'd take a look at their house here."

"If yer helping look for young Ariel, what are you doing here on Pender Island with your own daughter?"

Fair question.

"I got a lead that the kidnappers may have been to the island recently. I brought my daughter because I'm a single father."

"To a place where kidnappers could be?"

Fairer question.

"I had no choice." I leave it at that.

He lowers the gun. It's no longer pointing where it could remove my head though it could easily shred my lower half.

"OK. You've seen it. You can leave."

I turn and, not taking my eyes off him, I sidle over to the truck and get in. The driveway connects to a paved circle in front of the garage. I use it to turn and drive off.

"Are you OK Ell?" I ask as we move under the tree canopy.

"Why was that man pointing a gun at you Daddy?"

"He thought I might be a burglar. He looks after that house."

"Oh, OK. Are we going for dinner now?"

I give her a bigger smile than I feel. "We sure are."

I pull off the driveway onto the road and head back the way we came. At the end of the road I signal right. There is a restaurant about a half mile away. As I look to the left for any oncoming traffic, I notice the street sign. For the second time today, the hairs on the back of my neck stand up. This changes everything and, again, I don't know what it means. But two things I do know: I will find out and I'm going to call Arnold as soon as we get to the restaurant.

————

ARNOLD IS NOT one for praise so his "Very well done, Mr. Rogan. It could be a coincidence but I think not" felt good. He will look into the matter further. As will I.

After the initial rush at the discovery, I have settled down to a nice dinner with Ellie. Tomorrow we will go to the last marina to see if anyone recognizes the boat, but for now we're just going to have fun.

It's a family-style restaurant which, Ellie was delighted to discover, served her current favorite restaurant food: chicken strips and fries. I settled for the Salisbury steak which is better than I expected and I'm allowing myself one celebratory beer.

"I like eating in restaurants," says Ellie as she dips a fry deep into her ketchup. "Two in one day. I like this one better than the one at lunch."

"Me too." Another mouthful of IPA descends into my stomach.

"I went to a restaurant with Mommy and her friend."

"I know sweetie. Mommy told me. Did you like it?"

"No. They didn't have anything I liked." The silly, jealous part of me is glad that Edward Perot couldn't take Ellie to a place that she liked.

"Do you know what Daddy?"

"What sweetie?"

"They had rabbit on the menu. That is sooooooo mean."

Rabbit? Not many places in Vancouver serve it. It must have been expensive.

"What was the name of the restaurant?"

"It was a silly name. I wouldn't have remembered it except that Mommy's friend kept talking about it."

"What was it?"

When she tells me, I chuckle at the coincidence, then as I remember what Sam said, combined with three words in a calendar, electricity fires through my spine for the third time in an hour.

Everything, but everything, has been turned on its head.

34

SAM

I'm so glad you were free this evening. I was surprised." He has an open, friendly face. As he looks at me, it makes me feel like I am the only person in the world and that he is completely focused on me. It is no wonder that he's such a success as a politician.

"Me too," I say with a grin. "I was surprised that you asked me after the fuss Ellie made over dinner the other night."

He chuckles. "I don't blame her. Anywhere that doesn't serve chicken strips and fries doesn't deserve a great customer like her."

"That's kind of you to say that. Do you have children?"

"Unfortunately not. My late wife and I tried but..." He leaves it hanging.

"Well it's never too late." I smile. Then I realize the implication and feel a blush ascending into my cheeks.

"Well who knows," he says with the raise of an eyebrow which makes him look very sexy. It makes me feel a lot better; I wonder if that means... Oh stop Sam! There I go, getting ahead of myself again. "Ellie seems like a very well brought up young lady. You should be very proud of her."

"I am." I smile, the embarrassment has passed.

"What are her interests? Other than chicken strips and fries."

"She loves math and science. She has a small group of friends she likes to socialize with and when she grows up she wants to be a detective."

"A det—?" his sentence is cut off by the buzzing of his phone. He looks down at it and his smile fades. Before I can look at it he has picked it up from the table. "I'm so sorry," he says, "a politician's life is not his own. Do you mind?"

"No, of course not."

He stands and talks into the phone, "Ed Perot." He walks out on the restaurant's patio and listens to what the caller is saying. He occasionally says a word to two and a worried look has come over his face. Although I can't hear what he's saying I feel like an eavesdropper. I bury my nose in the menu. Mmm, they have Osso Bucco, I wonder if it's as good as mine. Cal says mine's the best in the world. Cal, what are you doing in my mind again? The miso salmon in phyllo sounds quite wonderful. I think I'll have that or the chicken penne.

"Sorry about that," he sits back down and smiles although the look of worry hasn't completely left his face. "I'll switch it off." He shuts off his phone and puts it in a pocket. That was a nice gesture.

"So tell me all about Ellie."

Like every parent I never miss a chance to sing the praises of my child. I do so for what seems altogether too long a time but he seems attentive and interested, so I finally wind it up.

"She sounds marvelous. I have a favorite niece who sounds just like her; she loves ballet. Does Ellie like to dance?"

I remember Ellie's cavorting in parody of the *Canada's Littlest Beauty* show and chuckle. "Well she certainly is enthusiastic in that department but probably needs some lessons." I love that he's interested in Ellie but I really want him to ask about me.

"Where is she tonight, with a babysitter?"

"No. She has gone with her father to Pender Island." His face looks a little, I don't know, puzzled? I wonder what that means. Still, it's given me time to change the subject so I ask, "Was it difficult to go from business to politics?"

He smiles a little ruefully, "Oh yes. They are very different worlds. In business, you know how you are doing by the numbers. If you make your company profitable you're doing well. But in politics, it's a lot less straightforward. You seem to have so many masters. It makes for strange, shall we say, bedfellows." Again that rather sexy raised eyebrow, is he coming on to me? I do kind of hope so.

If I had to guess, I would say that he misses his old life as a businessman.

"But never mind all that," he says pulling a broad grin back onto his face, "tell me about you. I know you're a talented photographer and a great designer but that's about all…" his voice trails off. He is looking over my left shoulder and the look of worry has returned. Except that it's not worry. I think it's fear.

"Excuse me a moment," he says and gets up. A young man has come up to the table. He is quite tall, rather handsome and well dressed. I think I've seen his face somewhere before. He takes a long look at me and I feel a wave of fear rollover me followed by relief when he turns back to Ed.

He has a bulky envelope in his hand which he hands over.

"You know what this is for?" he asks.

Ed nods and takes it.

"OK then." He turns and walks off, his showy snakeskin boots making an irritatingly loud noise on the restaurant's parquet flooring.

———

APART from the intrusion of the messenger with the envelope, it has been a wonderful evening. Ed and I have found a whole host of things in common and his interest in Ellie and her comings and goings is endearing. He is interesting without being dangerous like Cal.

He opens the door of his Jaguar for me and takes my hand to help me out. It's a little old-fashioned but I really like it. And he doesn't let go as he walks me to my front door. He holds on to my hand as we climb the steps. Our conversation has ranged over a wide variety of topics and the combination of good food, fine wine and his undoubted charm and sexiness has emboldened me to follow through on the decision I made halfway through dessert. "Would you like to come in for coffee and a nightcap?"

He takes my other hand and looks deep into my eyes. "Are you sure?"

Holding tightly to his hands, I stand on tiptoes and give him a gentle kiss on the cheek. "Very sure."

His face has turned very serious. "Then I would like that very much."

I reach in my purse and with a slightly trembling hand, I unlock the door and lead him inside.

35

CAL

SATURDAY

W e are in a diner on Pender Island where Ellie is delighted with the breakfast menu. As I watch her with what I know is a silly parental smile on my face, I can't help thinking of Ariel. I wonder if she is alive and if, on the unlikely chance that she is alive, what she might be doing. But I can't think about that. I have to assume she is alive and I have to find her.

"Waffles with blueberries!" Ellie announces her choice.

I signal the server to come over. She gives me the one-finger-raised-with-a-smile signal that says she'll be right there.

Our trip to Pender Island has been fun but although I have learned something stunning about Dave Bradbury, I am still no closer to finding Ariel. My hopes that someone might recognize Sherri Oliver, or the boat on which she sped away from this island last Thursday, have been dashed. I can't help thinking about that poor kid. Every time I think of her I am suffused with anger at myself for losing the one lead we had: Sherri Oliver. I know I would do anything to save her yet I didn't do the one thing that would have: cooperate with Steve and the VPD.

"What's the matter Daddy? You look sad. Were you thinking about Ariel?" I am shocked at the combination of observation and intuition in my daughter.

"Wow, Ell, you would be a great detective."

"I'm going to be, just like you," she answers proudly before a cloud crosses her face. "Whoops, Mommy told me not to tell you that."

"That's OK sweetie." Why would Sam tell her that?

"Hi are you ready to order?" the fresh-faced server asks us.

"Waffles and blueberries, please. And a glass of milk."

"I'll have the 'Full Works' breakfast and coffee, please." I don't usually eat breakfast but I'm going to go with Ellie's holiday spirit.

"I'm glad that you want to be a detective Ell and I'm going to give you some advice that my Mom gave me when I was young. You have to work hard in school and get at least one University degree before you become a policewoman."

"OK, Daddy."

"Maybe you could get a degree in Forensic Science. That's where you use science to discover how someone did a crime and who did it."

"Are you using that to find Ariel?"

"No sweetie."

"Why not?" Why not indeed. She is asking great questions.

"You know what? You *would* be a good detective, you know all the right questions to ask." That elicits a big smile. That smile, for a joyous moment, drives away my cares and worries. "*Bring me a father that so loved his child, Whose joy of her is overwhelming like mine,*" I misquote. "That was one of the things I learned in University."

The moment of joy has freed my mind. Maybe I have got closer to finding Ariel. The Bradbury home on Pender Island is on Razor Point Road. It's the same name as the company that sent the blackmail money to try and get Larry Corliss to quit the race for Mayor. We speculated that it might be drug money. If Bradbury controls the money maybe Ariel's kidnapping is being used to control him. It might explain why he hasn't seemed concerned about her disappearance. He knows if he does what he's told he'll get her back. There are a few too many ifs, mights and maybes but it's definitely worth pursuing.

"Thank you my darling girl. You just gave me a clue."

"You're welcome."

I can't help feeling a little stirring of pride at the thought that Ellie wants to be a detective 'just like me'. Hopefully she'll be a better one.

36

ARIEL

No more dancing lessons. No more dressing up. If only I could be with Mommy and Daddy. I've been here for like forever. The kind old lady who doesn't speak English is taking me for a walk in the garden. It's very pretty and soooooo big. We are near what that policewoman calls the beach. But it's not like any beach I've ever seen. It's all rocky and it hurts my feet when I walk on it. And there's that wooden dock thing. It like floats on the water and that pretty boat is tied up to it.

The policewoman said that I just have to give one performance then I can go home. She said it's real soon. I hope it is. I really want to see Mommy and Daddy. I miss them so much.

The nice lady looks up in the air and I hear the sound. I don't like it because every time it's brought that man who just looks at me. He's yucky.

I can see it now. The black helicopter. It's really loud too. It's landing way over the other side of the garden.

I hope he's not in it.

I really, really, really hope he's not.

37

SAM

Cal texted to say they will be here soon. I can't wait to see them. Seeing Ellie will be wonderful and will make me feel so much better. However, the thoughts of Cal have me confused. I keep going over it again and again.

Ed Perot and I had a lovely evening. When he got back here we had coffee and liqueurs and he wanted to see my photo portfolios. He thought my pictures of Ellie were wonderful and he was so attentive. When he looked like he was about to kiss me, I slid closer to him on the couch but he didn't respond so I thought that maybe he was shy or maybe I was the first person he had got close to since the death of his wife and so I decided to make it easier for him.

I topped up his glass then excused myself and went into the bedroom, primped, put on my sexiest negligée and came out. He was standing, sorting through my photos so I walked over and put my arms around his neck. I was immediately turned on by the feel of his hardness through the thin silk. He looked into my eyes the way he did in the restaurant and I just melted inside.

Then he just mumbled, "I'm sorry. I can't." And he left.

I was stunned.

He left me feeling like I was dirty. How could I have read him so badly? Clearly he was turned on but... Did I do something wrong? Maybe the perfume I dabbed across my throat made him think of his dead wife. Maybe I was going too fast for him. I just don't know. But I can't shake this feeling of dirtiness. And thinking of Cal about to arrive makes it feel worse and I really don't know why.

The madly ringing doorbell drags me out of my thoughts but not out of my mood. I can hear Ellie's chatter as I go to the door. What would she think? And will the ever-observant Cal divine my thoughts?

I open the door.

"Mommy, you will *never* guess what we saw from the plane. We saw killer whales and they were so close. There was even a baby one, he was sooooo cute." My spirits are immediately lifted and I wish I could pick her up and twirl her around but the MS has put an end to that.

Instead I hug her. I look up and see Cal standing, uncertain, in the doorway. "Come in then," I tell him.

"How was your trip?" I ask Ellie but get the reply, "I have to go pee *really* badly." She scoots off into the powder room.

Cal is standing there like a shy schoolboy. "So, how was the trip?" I ask him.

"It was great. We had such a fun time. I had some business to look into as well and she was really patient. We got to see all of the Island, explored the beach, had some great food and just generally had a perfect father-daughter time."

My spirits are doubly lifted.

"Were you looking for clues to Ariel Bradbury's disappearance?"

"Yes. We went round to all the harbors and marinas looking for a boat that I think her kidnapper owns. Ell loved seeing all the boats and the fishermen on the docks. She's inquisitive about everything."

"Did you find the boat you were looking for?"

His expression sobers a bit. "No, but I did find a connection that might be relevant, I'm going to check it out later."

"That's good. It's progress, right?"

"I guess." I can see his mind chewing over what he learned.

Suddenly I don't want him to go. "Why don't you stay for a bit and have a coffee?"

"Sorry, I can't. I have to meet with Arnold and then I promised Nick I'd help him on a case he's working on."

"Well how about dinner? We could send out to Bella Pizza." Am I sounding too eager?

"Sorry, there's a lead I have to follow and I can only do it tonight. It's connected to the Ariel case."

"Oh." I feel deflated again. I want to ask him if maybe tomorrow night would work but I don't want to sound needy.

"I'd better get going. Arnold's expecting me in about ten minutes and I'm fifteen minutes from his office."

He shouts a goodbye to Ell and leaves me alone with my thoughts. Cal made me think that maybe we could be a family again. I'm pretty sure he hasn't used since the time he was kidnapped and shot full of drugs. And somehow this private detective business with Nick seems to be working out.

And he is such a good man. He always wants to do good and I can't imagine that will ever change.

Maybe the thing with Ed Perot worked out the way it was supposed to.

I'll tidy up a bit and then take Ell shopping. As I walk to the bookcase, I can see my portfolio of Ellie's pics is open on the coffee table. A reminder of last night which I need to erase. The pictures are a complete mess, not in their previous order. Cal always used to laugh at my fussiness about the arrangement of my picture portfolios. As I rearrange them I smile, thinking about the circumstances of each shot. After her first day of school, her first time in the St. Cecelia's uniform, her first big gymnastics competition. Some of the pictures seem to be missing. I'm sure I saw them last night. Maybe they are in the wrong place.

I sort through them; at least three of them are gone; if memory serves they were pictures I took of her in her swim-suit on Second Beach. Did Ed put them somewhere? I have to sort these out and find the missing ones. They must be here somewhere. But where?

38

CAL

M y phone beeps. Great, it's the email from Steve. The attachment is a one-page WORD document. I read it.

I know what you've been doing, $100,000 will buy my silence.

If you pay me $100,000 I will destroy the evidence.

I know what you did. I have the evidence. A payment of $100,000 is nothing to you. I will give you the evidence when you give me the money. Must be a public place.

Its lack of specificity is annoying. It's like Mark Traynor was scripting various ways of presenting his blackmail pitch. It could apply to Thomas Radcliffe but despite what I learned from Adriana his secretary, I'm betting not. I'll know better tonight.

"Mr. Rogan, come in and sit down."

I get up and walk into Arnold's office. As always he comes straight to the point.

"When we took on Larry Corliss as a client we did checks on everybody connected to his campaign and the campaign of Edward Perot. That was when I discovered that David Bradbury's company was teetering on the edge of bankruptcy. It didn't seem germane at the time. However, we didn't look into the affairs of his wife. So we knew nothing of her property on Pender Island, on Razor Point Road as you discovered. It can hardly be a coincidence that the Cayman Islands company which paid Mr. Corliss a cool quarter of a million for withdrawing from the race is called Razor Point Holdings. Mr. Bradbury supplied the money to get Mr. Corliss out of the race."

"We've been assuming that it was a drug gang that wanted Larry out of the race," I say. A frown passes across Arnold's face; is it because of my use of Corliss' first name or is it something else? "Maybe this has nothing to do with drugs."

"I'm not so sure. I've had some time to think about this and make some discreet inquiries. Here's what I think happened." Arnold looks like a cat who has just found a bowl of cream. "After your call yesterday, I have looked into the affairs of Bentley and Bradbury a little more deeply. It's a private firm so its financial statements are not public, however after a lot of digging I discovered that the firm was initially capitalized to the tune of almost a hundred million dollars by Mrs. Bradbury's father just before his death. Bradbury invested that money into a number of companies in such diverse fields as mining, oil and gas exploration and high-tech. Interestingly, all the companies in which he invested over a period of years went into bankruptcy. I have people digging deeper but I think those companies were just shells, controlled by him, that allowed him to funnel the Bradbury wealth into his own pockets."

"Thieving bastard," is all I can think to say.

"Oh but that's not the half of it," says Arnold in his most British of tones. "It seems that there was a very substantial investment made in Bentley and Bradbury a few years back. And this was also invested in a number of little known companies which all similarly went bankrupt. But those companies most likely made payments to phony suppliers by check or bank transfer."

"Money laundering!"

"Indeed. I think Mr. Bradbury is in cahoots with a drug gang. So while my people dig into the financial side. Your job is to (a) prove Bradbury's connection to drugs and (b) turn Bradbury. With Bradbury on our side, Larry Corliss can reveal that he was blackmailed and return to the race to be MP for Vancouver East. And we can hand Bradbury over to the VPD; they can use him to get to Santiago."

"What about Ed Perot? What if Bradbury has contributed to his re-election as a proxy for Santiago." I ask.

"Yes, I've been mulling that over too. I think Mr. Perot is a decent man. I doubt that he knows the source of Bradbury's wealth. Nevertheless, you have to look into it."

Oh I will Arnold. You don't know how much yet.

Arnold stands. Meeting over. Unexpectedly he shakes my hand before ushering me out.

As I leave his office, *I* feel like the cat who got the bowl of cream. I've got two tasks to perform and I'm looking forward to them both.

39

CAL

Pigeon Park. It's a total misnomer: a triangle of sidewalk on the corner of Hastings and Carrall teeming as usual with the dispossessed of the downtown east side. People in ragged clothing, eking out a living selling single cigarettes, crackheads jabbering and twitching and trying to figure out where the next hit is coming from, an addict on the nod enjoying the fading ecstasy of her recent hit of heroin or, god forbid, fentanyl. This is the place I used to call home. It's not far from where the Mayor, Council and City officials of 1886 pitched a tent and labeled it 'City Hall.' We've come a long way baby but not all of it is good. This is my city at its ugliest.

I'm here to fulfill my promise to Stammo to help on the Tyler case. I don't want to be here. It stirs up the Beast inside who is dying for a hit of heroin. I can't seem to escape it. The best part of the Ariel Bradbury case was that there was no drug connection but with the discovery that Dave Bradbury probably controls the company that paid off Larry Corliss, even that is gone. I can't seem to get away from it.

Right now I want to be grilling Bradbury about Razor Point Holdings, but Stammo is not letting me off the hook.

Anyway, his plan may be pretty damn drastic but it makes sense.

I look east on Hastings and see Stammo's van parked by the curb in the next block. He must have the window cracked open because periodically a stream of smoke appears from the driver's side. He's nervous. These days he only smokes when he's nervous. His snitch, Eddie, told him that Tyler comes here to deliver drugs to the flophouse which the gangs deal out of every day around noon. I check my watch for the tenth time. Ten past twelve, three minutes later than the last time I checked.

"Looking to buy?" With that unerring instinct of an addict he knows I might be a customer. He's probably around twenty-five but looks decades older.

"Got any white stuff?" I find myself asking and suddenly the longing washes through me.

"Sure. Fifteen bucks."

Without thinking, I reach for my wallet and the cash and baggie are exchanged in that furtive way we are both all too familiar with. He turns and walks quickly away as I pocket the heroin.

I look around guiltily to see if Stammo observed the transaction when I notice a Mercedes SUV pull up on Carrall street. This'll be him. No one in a Mercedes stops their vehicle at Pigeon Park. I feel the thrill of anticipation. The call to action.

A young-ish guy gets out of the driver's seat. It's not Tyler. Maybe someone else is making the drop. I can't see him that well, he's shielded by the Merc. He moves to the back and the hatchback door opens. I can see him now. Well-dressed, confident looking. He reminds me of the long-dead Blondie from my past.

He reaches into the back and takes out a big aluminum baking pan. He carries it over to one of the benches and deposits it there. "Help yourselves," he says.

People descend on the free food like pigeons on a slice of bread. "Thanks, man." "God bless you." "You're doin' a real good thing, sir." The voices ring out, truly grateful for this small act of kindness. No sign of jealousy or resentment that a rich guy in a fancy car is dispensing charity. The man nods and smiles, almost shyly, as he gets back into his SUV and drives off.

People walk away from the baking pan with handfuls of chicken wings, handing some to their friends in wheelchairs, enjoying what may be their only meal of the day. One raggedy old guy nudges the heroin addict. Her eyes open blearily and he pushes some chicken into her hand: a man with nothing, giving something.

The burble of a car exhaust catches my attention. There it is, pulling up on the Hastings Street edge of the park. A blue Shelby. I sit down on a bench so that I can look inside. The passenger door opens and Tyler gets out, looking exactly like Stammo's photo of him with the small birthmark on his chin. He reaches behind the seat and takes out a metal briefcase. The drugs. As he steps back I get a good look at the driver. Young, well-dressed, good-looking. Not a lot different from the Good Samaritan in the Mercedes, on the surface anyway. More to the point, I recognize him. I feel a touch of smugness. I'm betting that if I could see his feet, they would be encased in expensive snakeskin boots. He's the same guy whom we ejected from the debate between Larry Corliss and Edward Perot. At the time, something deep in my consciousness figured that he was the Bookman. I'm still wondering how he knew my name. And if he knows *my* name does he know about Sam and Ellie? A worm of fear slithers through my gut.

Just like Eddie, Stammo's snitch, told us was the routine, the Bookman drives off with a little squeal of the tires. I get up and head off Tyler on his path to the flophouse.

"Tyler?" I say. He looks at me, his blue eyes neutral. Even

though his boss knows me, he shows zero signs of recognition.

"Yeah," he says.

I see Stammo's van pull into the space vacated by the Shelby. I nod in its direction and say, "He wants to talk to you."

He turns and watches as the passenger window slides down revealing Stammo, cigarette gone, leaning across the passenger seat toward him. "Come here a minute, Tyler," he says.

I match Tyler's pace as he takes the three steps to the curb and leans into the window. "Hi Mr. Stammo." I can't see his face but can hear the hint of exasperation in his voice. "Listen, I know my Dad wants me to go back home but it just ain't gonna happen. I told you that before. I've got a life out here, I'm doing real good." The English major in me cringes at the grammar, but I ignore it and slide open the side door of Stammo's converted minivan.

"Just get inside and listen to what Mr. Stammo has to say." I feel my muscles tense.

He turns to me, suspicion wrought across his face. He glances at Stammo and knows exactly what's happening. Instinct and adrenaline take over but before he can move, my right hand has grabbed his bicep and pulled him off balance and toward the van door. He partly recovers but I'm too quick. I reach across him with my left hand and grab the lapel of his leather jacket; I spin him toward me and give him a mighty shove and lift, depositing him on his back on the floor of the van.

I scoop up his legs, push them inside the van and my world explodes in a galaxy of stars.

I look up from the sidewalk and through the blur I can just see my assailant. A big guy, straggly hair, beer belly and tattoos. Stammo's description of Carl: gang member, drug dealer, thug. He is pulling Tyler out of the van. He must think that he has incapacitated me. Almost without thought, my leg scythes into the back of his left knee and he stumbles forward undoing his efforts to extricate Tyler. By the time I'm on my feet, he has recovered and turned to face me, just in time to stop my fist with his fleshy nose. It's a hasty punch without a lot of force and he bellows more from annoyance than pain.

"Fight!" I hear from one of the people behind me. There are a few cheers. I'm the lunchtime entertainment.

I follow my first jab with a hard right to the head; it has Carl staggering but before I can follow through, Tyler aims a kick at my crotch. Rookie move. I pivot and cup my hand under his calf and flip him back into the van. It gives me maybe three seconds and as I turn back toward Carl, I see it. A black hunting knife. Just like Roy used to carry and is now buried with.

He has a big gloating smile on his face. "I'm gonna cut you, you son of a—" Another error made. His gloating time has given me the opportunity to plant myself sideways and as he steps forward my right leg curls up and releases, slamming my heel into his knee. Not quite enough force to break but enough to incapacitate for a few moments. Through the battle mist, I hear an approving roar from the crowd and feel a leather-clad arm across my throat. Tyler is stronger than I expected and he is holding on for all he's worth, no doubt hoping to slow me down while Carl takes the time to recover. It takes me a second or two to swing around then I'm in position. I have been pulling forward against the arm so now I reverse and back-pedal, slamming Tyler into the side of Stammo's van, letting my head snap back. I'm a couple of inches taller than him so the back of my head doesn't connect with his nose but it has certainly increased the momentum of his head as it connects with the opened door. His arm on my throat loosens enough to allow me to wriggle free and turn toward Carl.

Carl's not there. But there is a uniformed policeman,

almost exactly my height and build but much younger and I'm betting much fitter. His nightstick is raised ready to strike. I think that if this were somewhere other than Canada, I might have been shot already. I raise my hands and step back.

The world slows to normal. I figure that not more than twenty seconds have passed since I slid open the door of the minivan. How did the cop get here so quickly? I look around. Standing to my right with his hand on his holstered Glock is Sarge. An old-timer at the VPD with whom I have some history. Much of it not good.

The young cop speaks first. "All of you, hands on the van." Tyler, Carl and I all obey.

Within seconds, we all have our hands cuffed behind us with plastic zip ties.

I'm guessing it's going to be some hours before we can sort all this out; precious hours that are keeping me from getting closer to finding Ariel.

Then it hits me. I have a baggy of heroin in my pocket. When we get to the Cambie Street Station that is going to complicate matters a lot.

Stammo has wheeled down the ramp from his van and is sitting next to me while the uniforms are calling for backup. In deference to their former working relationship, Sarge hasn't cuffed him.

"Nick, I need you to do something for me."

"Sure, anything."

I'm going to rely on the guilty feelings he must have about the situation we are now in. "In my pocket there's a baggie. Can you take it out."

He cuts me a sharp look which quickly morphs into disgust. He looks over at the uniforms and, shaking his head in disapproval, slips his hand into my pocket. He pulls out the baggy and flicks it behind him into the gutter. The wrench I feel is greater than the relief. I try to console myself with the thought that most of the heroin now sold in Vancouver is not heroin at all but fentanyl and that it may very well have killed me.

But even that thought doesn't make me feel any better.

And to make matters worse, this fiasco is going to take up precious time I could be spending tracking down Ariel.

40

STAMMO

W hat the fuck, Mr. Stammo?" He glares at me through the bars. "You tried to fuckin' *kidnap* me. D'you think I was just gonna go back to Toron'o like some little kid going home to Mommy and Daddy. Now I'm in here with my fingerprints all over a brief-case with a kilo of coke in it. What the fuck?"

He's right. And Rogan was right too. He only went ahead with the kidnapping idea because I persuaded him. We finally sorted the whole thing out and Rogan's gone off to follow up his lead on the Ariel kidnapping. To his credit, he didn't blame me for the whole damn thing, not out loud anyway.

"Look Tyler I'm sorry. But maybe—"

"Sorry! You're sorry! I'm gonna go to jail for god knows how many years and you're fucking sorry. Oh, well that's OK isn't it."

I wonder how I'm going to tell his Dad that I'm the reason his son's in jail. Oh God.

"You're not gonna go to jail, Ty."

That stops him. I can see the anger leave his face a bit.

"What'ja mean?" There is hope there. Not much but some.

"A plea bargain. No time and witness protection. All

you've got to do is tell them that you worked for this Bookman character and for Carlos Santiago."

"But Mr. Stammo, you don't understand—"

"Sure I do. Look, I'll even pay for the lawyer out of my own pocket. I know a great one. James Garry. He demolished me on the stand quite a few times, I hated the bastard but he is one hell of a defense lawyer." I'm not sure how I'm gonna come up with the money. Conscience money is what it is.

He goes quiet. "Do you think I could, like, not have to go to prison?"

"Sure. Now listen carefully. Do not say anything to anyone until you've spoken to the lawyer. Promise me."

"Sure, I promise. But there's one thing I need to tell you—"

"No!" I interrupt him. "Don't tell me anything, OK. I can be forced to repeat something you said to me but your lawyer can't. Like I said, say nothing 'til you've spoken with him."

"OK, Mr. Stammo." He kinda deflates, poor kid.

Now I've got to go home and face the music with Bob, his Dad. It's not gonna be pretty.

Hopefully Rogan is gonna have a more productive evening.

41

CAL

I sure am glad they have a bar here. With nothing on the menu under thirty bucks I'm glad I don't have to freak out Stammo with a huge expense claim. I've already freaked him out enough today—not that it wouldn't be worth it. Mark Traynor's calendar had an entry for last Thursday at seven: a line of dollar signs followed by the words The Lift. The same restaurant and the same time where Edward Perot came with Sam and Ellie, ostensibly because he had a meeting scheduled here which was canceled. A coincidence perhaps? Perhaps not.

The view is spectacular. Vancouver Harbor in the foreground with its marinas and boathouses, the Stanley Park rainforest to my left and the North Shore Mountains behind still capped with snow which may not melt until as late as June or July. This is my city at its most beautiful. I regret that it's too cold to sit out on the deck.

Another big plus is that they have a well-curated selection of local craft beer. I'm enjoying a hazy IPA with the interesting brand name of Trash Panda. It's a lovely local beer and it's helping me forget the Tyler fiasco—which used up all of the

ROBERT P. FRENCH

afternoon—even if my aching body keeps reminding me I'm forty and too damned old for fighting gang members.

"Great selection of beer here," I say to the barman. That sends him off on a long diatribe about the beer scene. Vancouverites are big craft beer fans. I join in with as many encouraging words as I can and soon we are like old buddies. When he finally runs out of steam, I extend my hand. "Cal," I say. He reciprocates, "Josh."

We chat some more, this time about hockey and the upcoming Stanley Cup playoffs; his favorite subject, not mine. Eventually, I think I'm at the right place in the conversation.

I take the folder out of my briefcase and slide out a photo. "Hey Josh, d'you know this guy?"

"Sure. Edward Perot, he's running for the federal seat in my 'hood. He comes here a lot. Good guy, but I'm a Corliss man."

"Did you see him here last Tuesday?"

He thinks for a bit. "Sure. That was the evening the Canucks got trashed. I was working here so I missed the game. He was here with a cute woman and a little kid." I feel that flush of jealousy about Sam being out with him, even if Ellie was a de facto chaperone. My smile fades as Josh's gaze focuses over my right shoulder and the smile fades from *his* face.

The voice could not be described as anything other than prissy. "Excuse me sir."

I swivel toward him.

"I'm pleased to say that we guard our patron's privacy. None of our staff," he pauses and gives a lemon-sour smile at Josh, "are allowed to divulge client information."

Well, good for you, but I don't give up that easily. I pull a business card from the breast pocket of my jacket and hand it to him. "I'm working closely with the police on the disappearance of a child and I think you may have some information that's vital. You could speak to me now or I could call the police and have them come over and interrogate you later this evening... when you're busier."

He looks me straight in the eye. "Why don't you do that, sir. However, until they arrive, I'm afraid I'm going to have to ask you to leave." I misjudged him. But I can't let this go. If I get this right I'm going to be one step closer to finding Ariel. She's been missing for eight long days I've got to try another tack.

"Please. This little girl has been missing for over a week. Her parents are beside themselves with worry. You really could be very helpful."

"Oh. Well, that's different. I would be happy to help in any way I can. As soon as the police arrive I'll tell them *anything* they need to know. Meanwhile..." He inclines his head toward the door. "No need to pay for the drink; it's on us." His smile is as warm as a penguin's rear end.

————

THE TEMPERATURE HAS DROPPED to just above freezing and the Healey's English heater is not really up to it. The manager is long gone and I'm waiting in the carpark for Josh the barman to head off home.

Finally he appears. I jump out of the car and trot over to him. "Hey, Josh."

"Oh hi," he says. He looks over my shoulder. "Is that yours?"

"Yeah."

"What year?"

"'63 it's a Mark II." I say with pride.

"Sweet."

"I hope you didn't get in trouble with your manager."

"Nah. He and I don't usually see eye-to-eye but we manage to coexist."

"I know he's big into client privacy and I respect that. But there's a little girl's life on the line here."

He looks around. "Sure. Let's go to the St. Regis. They're open 'til two. It'll be a bit warmer than standing out here and I'd like a ride in an Austin Healey 3000 anyway.

Ah, the joys of good beer, English sports cars and late-hours bars.

———

THE WARMTH of the bar is settling into my bones and the Yellow Dog IPA is settling into my stomach. It provokes a shard of guilt: I'm here in comfort and Ariel is out there somewhere, desperate to be home again.

I open my folder. Perot's picture is on the top of the pile. Josh is excited. He's never talked to a private investigator before and I told him as much as I could of the Ariel Bradbury case on the way here. He's primed to help. Mindful that I might need to swear to this in court, I spread all my photographs on the table. "Apart from Mr. Perot, are there any other faces you recognize?"

His gaze goes to Sherri Oliver. He taps the picture. "I'd like to know her but unfortunately…" He points to another. "That's Larry Corliss. I was going to vote for him. Any idea why he bailed?" I shake my head. He shrugs and points to Mark Traynor and I hold my breath. Finally, "I've seen him. He came in about two weeks ago. No, wait a minute, it was Friday the sixth." I try not to show my surprise. That was the day Ariel went missing. I'm not sure if it's relevant. Yet.

"Did he come in with anyone?"

"No he was alone." Damn. Before I can ask him my next question he continues, "I remember it was Friday because Mr. Perot was in having a meal with three other gentlemen. They seemed to be celebrating something. They got through three bottles of Billecart Salmon at four hundred bucks a pop."

I really have to try to keep the excitement out of my voice. "Josh, this is very important. Did this man talk to Perot?"

"Yeah, yeah, he did. He paid his bar tab and walked over and seemed to whisper something in Mr. Perot's ear. Mr. Perot got up and they went outside on to the patio. It was a cold evening so the patio was empty. They were out there for a while and when they came back in, the guy left right away."

"How did Perot act when he came back in?"

"I couldn't tell really. We were slammed, you know, Friday night. But he left early before the others. He didn't seem too happy then."

I breathe a deep sigh. I think my hunch was right. Mark Traynor was blackmailing Perot, then five days later he turns up dead. But what did Traynor have on Perot?

"Thanks Josh. You don't know how helpful you've been." I 'Cheers' him and call over the waiter. As he's taking the order for two more, Josh shuffles through the other photos. "I know this guy too, he was with Mr. Perot that Friday night. He was the one who picked up the bill. It was over two grand with the tip."

He's pointing at Dave Bradbury.

I ask myself again why the hell would Bradbury be out celebrating with Perot on the day his daughter was kidnapped.

42

CAL

SUNDAY

I want to speak to Dave Bradbury about Razor Point Holdings but after my meeting last night with Josh, the barman at The Lift, I have to explore something else first. When I first saw Radcliffe, I thought he looked more like a student than a TV producer. Now he just looks like hell. The Pre-Trial Correctional Center will do that to someone. Good. Anyone who makes kiddy-porn deserves everything he gets. Wait until he gets to Fraser Regional after he's found guilty, that's going to be a *lot* more unpleasant. Better.

But I don't show any of that on my face. "How are you doing Mr. Radcliffe?" I ask.

"How the fuck do you think?" He gestures at the grim surroundings in anger. Let me stoke that up a bit.

"I spoke to your secretary, Adriana." A hint of fear joins the anger on his face. Good, lots of emotion. "I'm sorry to tell you that she recanted her alibi for the time of Mark's murder."

Now the fear takes over. "You didn't tell the police did you?" he's begging now.

"I'm afraid I had to." True. It was my key to getting Steve to give me authorization to be here.

He deflates. All the emotions sigh out of him. "But I didn't kill him," a note of pleading creeps into his voice. "You have to believe me." He looks into my eyes. "Please."

I'm enjoying this way too much.

"As a matter of fact…" I leave it hanging for a beat. "I do believe you Mr. Radcliffe."

"Oh, thank God, thank God," the words tumble out of him. "Do you have evidence? Can you get me off? I can pay, you know. You're a private detective, I know that, I can certainly pay your fees and if you—"

I cut him off. "You just need to answer some questions."

He pulls himself together. "Anything." I love the eagerness in his voice.

"OK," I smile at him. "First you need to know that the police have you dead to rights on the pornography charges, so anything you tell me now that might incriminate you on those charges is not going to make a difference. You understand that right?"

He nods.

"But if you help me now and your evidence brings a murderer to justice, then the Crown Prosecutor is more likely to give you a lighter sentence on the pornography charges."

"Anything."

"Mark blackmailed you into getting him a job on *Canada's Littlest Beauty* because he knew about your kiddy-porn movies right?" He nods again. "Do you think he might have been blackmailing anyone else?" I dare not lead him here; the name Perot has to come from him.

"Wouldn't surprise me. Mark was always looking for chances to make a quick buck."

"So think back to those days. Who else might Mark have tried to blackmail?"

"It could have been anyone. Anyone in the cast or the crew; we had a couple of cameramen, lighting people. Mark did the sound. There must have been ten or twelve people all told. It could be any of them."

He's opening up. "Could any of them afford to pay blackmail?"

He snorts. "Probably not. Most of 'em were film school students in need of a buck."

"It costs money to make a film. Who were the backers?"

"I put up fifty-one percent and got a couple of old pervs to put up the rest. They gave me the money on condition that they could watch the filming. They liked to watch thirteen year-olds... Well you know."

My stomach turns. "What are their names?" I ask.

"Doesn't matter. Mark wasn't blackmailing them." He laughs. It's not a nice laugh.

"How d'you know."

"Two years ago they both got busted and ended up in prison. One died and the other one's still inside."

"Anyone else you can think of?" I can hear a streak of desperation in my voice.

"No. I made great money on the first movie so I had enough to produce the others solo."

"Why'd you quit making them?"

"The market got weirder and weirder. People wanted stuff I wasn't prepared to do. Really young kids, rape, snuff, like that. I decided to go legit."

I try to block the thoughts coming into my mind. If I don't, I'll be throwing up.

"Where did you get the girls?" I ask. Not that it's relevant to what I need to know.

"You'd be surprised. Some were just precocious thirteen- and fourteen-year-old runaways. But some were there with their parents' permission. Go figure."

Despite my revulsion at his answer, a penny drops in my head. "Could Mark have been blackmailing one of those parents?"

He shrugs. "Sure. Why not?"

"Do you have a list of their names?"

"Yeah, they'll be in one of the files the police seized from my office I guess."

Maybe there'll be something. I'll see if I can get Steve to let me go through the files. Right now, I just want to get out of here away from this slime bucket. It won't be too many years until Ellie's thirteen. I can't imagine… I cut off the thoughts before they form pictures in my mind.

I need him to offer Perot as a likely mark for Traynor's blackmail.

I start to get up. "Pity you can't help me. I would have liked to help you."

"Wait. I had investors in *Beauty*. Mark would have known them. Maybe he was blackmailing one of them." He's desperate to help me in the hope of getting a lighter sentence.

"That was a legal business, why would he blackmail one of them?"

"I dunno. Maybe he saw something."

I sit down again.

"OK, who put up money for *Beauty*?"

"There was a guy called Milt Stafford and then Gabriel Schwartz—he's a big wheel in reality TV—and a couple of small players from out of town. But my biggest investor was a company. I never actually met anyone from it, it was all done by lawyers."

Well this has been a big waste of time. I so wanted him to volunteer a link between Mark and Perot. In a last ditch attempt I ask, "Did Mark ever mention that he knew Edward Perot, the MP?"

"Of course. Perot was on a government committee to boost the Canadian film and TV business. It was through him that I got the big investor. He's a good guy. Came by the set, every week."

My spine's on fire now.

"So Mark Traynor had contact with Perot?"

"Sure. Perot knew all the crew. He was always chatting with them. Typical politician, right? And he was really great with the kids and their parents." The fire in my spine is raging now though Radcliffe seems unaware of my excitement. "He would do little magic tricks for them, y'know make a quarter disappear and then pull it out of the kid's ear."

Radcliffe stops and for the first time sees the look on my face. "That's going to help, right?" he asks eagerly.

"Any of the families he particularly liked?" I ask.

"Well, he was always hanging around Rebecca Bradbury. Probably angling for a campaign donation, right? Don't get me wrong. He's a stand-up guy. He was really good to Mrs. Norton when…" His voice trails off and there's a shocked look on his face.

The name Norton rings a bell. "When what?" I ask.

"Nothing. I've said too much." he mumbles.

"If you want my help with the Crown Prosecutor, you'd better tell me right now."

He sighs. "When her daughter went missing."

That's it! When Stammo was looking into the Facebook page of the phony kid 'Justin' he discovered that he had been corresponding with another girl, a girl from Coquitlam, a girl who went missing. Her name was Norton. What was her first name?

Bingo! "Olivia Norton?" I ask.

"How d'you know that?"

I ignore his question. "Olivia Norton was a contestant on your show?"

"Yes, but—"

"And you say Perot was friendly. How friendly?"

"What do you mean how—?" He stops and looks at me. "Oh." We lock eyes. I don't move a muscle in my face; I just wait. "It's possible, I suppose." Is he telling me what he thinks I want to hear? "Sure, it's possible."

"You didn't see anything…" I leave it hanging.

"No. Nothing specific. He was very attentive to the kids, he'd, you know, push a stray hair behind an ear. Or give 'em a hug if they did a good job at something. I never thought of him as a perv and I've seen a few of them." In the mirror for one, I think. "But it's possible. For sure. Do you think Mark was blackmailing Perot?"

I ignore his question. "The company that invested in you, the one where you never met the people running it. Was it Razor Point Holdings?" I ask

"How the *hell* did you know that?"

Now I know everything. It all fits. I even think I know where Ariel is being held.

I get up. For once I'm eager to go and see Steve.

"Wait. So what I told you was useful, right?" Radcliffe bleats behind me. "You'll give a good report to the Crown Prosecutor about me. Help lighten my sentence."

I turn and look at him. He's a maker of kiddy-porn and, even worse, when I first questioned him about Ariel's disappearance he concealed the little matter of the disappearance of Olivia Norton.

I look him in the eye and force a smile onto my face though it feels more like a grimace. "Not a chance, buddy. I wouldn't piss on you if you were on fire."

I turn and walk out.

When I tell Steve what I know he'll get the full force of the Department to bust this case wide open.

I just pray that Ariel is still alive when we get there.

Then it hits me. There's one thing that doesn't fit. It's bothered me twice already but now it's an itch I don't have time to scratch.

43

STAMMO

Rogan has always been a keener, especially when he's making a breakthrough in a case. But it's not often I've seen him this wound up and ready to go. It's like every second's an hour of torture for him as we wait for Steve to join us in the conference room.

Graveley Street is a new building and I never spent much time here when I was still with the VPD but it still makes me feel the loss. Not just the job but the ability to walk in here just like any other cop. The hangover doesn't help much either, I spent far too much time with my old buddy Jim Beam after I spoke to Tyler's Dad last night.

Finally Steve makes his entrance and puts Cal out of his misery.

"So guys, what'ja got? It better be good getting me to come in here on a Sunday." he says as he sits down.

"Three things," Cal says. "We know who kidnapped Ariel and we know where she is, *and* we can hand you Carlos Santiago on a platter."

Talk about getting someone's attention. I'm betting Rogan practiced that little speech and it sure worked. Steve's eyes are as wide as they can go.

"OK, let's have it," he says.

"Ariel was on the show *Canada's Little Beauty*. Well, it just so happens that nine months ago, a kid from Coquitlam named Olivia Norton went missing and was never found. She had been a contestant on the previous season of the show but for some reason, someone in Coquitlam RCMP either dropped the ball or could never make a connection with the show."

"Are you saying Thomas Radcliffe is the kidnapper of these girls?"

"No. The girls were taken by a woman going by the name of Sherri Oliver; well, at least Ariel was. And when I questioned Radcliffe he gave me her name as someone he'd fired. He'd never have given me her name if he was involved."

Steve nods, he's heard this before but he's too savvy to say so and stop Cal's momentum.

Cal is smiling broadly; he's enjoying this. "Well it turns out that *Canada's Littlest Beauty* was financed in part by a company called Razor Point Holdings."

"What?!" I shout.

Two pairs of eyes turn to me. Cal's are frowning.

I can't keep the excitement out of my voice. "Razor Point Holdings is controlled by Carlos Santiago or at the least by one of his henchman, this mystery guy called the Bookman."

"How d'you know?" they say almost in unison.

"The Bookman drives a Shelby GT 350 and it's registered to…" It's my turn for the dramatic pause. "Razor Point Holdings."

"Perfect." Rogan's smile gets wider. "You see, Steve, this Razor Point holdings has come up in another context. You know I'm doing some work for Larry Corliss in his bid for the Vancouver East seat."

"Yes, but hasn't he withdrawn his candidacy?"

"He has, but only temporarily, and Steve, you've gotta keep that confidential. He was being blackmailed and he pretended to accept a bribe. When the bribe money came, it was paid by the same Razor Point Holdings."

"Sure," Steve jumps in. "I can see why Santiago would want to get rid of Corliss. Corliss is a big campaigner for drug legalization and that's the last thing Santiago wants. But are you saying Santiago is the kidnapper too?"

Cal doesn't answer directly but goes on, "The other big winner from Corliss' withdrawing from the race is Edward Perot. He's the incumbent in the seat for eight years and suddenly he's losing in the polls. But what's interesting is, Perot was the one who introduced Razor Point Holdings to *Canada's Littlest Beauty*. So Perot is in bed with Santiago."

"Why would Santiago launder money through a TV show?"

"He's not. You see on the strength of making the introduction, Perot would frequently drop by the set and chat with the girls. He was particularly close to Ariel and Olivia Norton. On my way up here, I stopped off to talk to the detectives who are combing through Thomas Radcliffe's books. They told me Razor Point only invested two hundred grand in the show. That's nothing to Santiago. I'm betting he did that as a favor to his buddy Perot to give him access."

"Access to what?"

"The little girls," Rogan says.

"Are you saying Perot's a pedophile?" Steve asks.

Rogan nods. "Yes and I think Mark Traynor knew and that he was blackmailing Perot. That's what got him killed. Another favor from Santiago."

"And the kidnapping?"

"I think Carlos Santiago is doing it and he's giving them as gifts to Perot."

"Sick fuck," I say. How anyone could do that to a kid? There's silence for a while.

"You know where he's keeping Ariel?" Steve asks.

"I think so. I tracked the phony policewoman Sherri

Oliver to an internet cafe on Salt Spring. She left there in a boat that went in the direction of Pender Island. So I also dropped in on the drug squad this morning. You had told me that Santiago had a villa in the Gulf Islands, they told me it's on Samuel Island, just a bit northeast of Pender Island. I'm betting that's where they're holding Ariel right now, if she's still alive.

"Steve, you need to get a warrant to search Santiago's property on Samuel Island."

Steve gets up and paces the room for a bit. Rogan is tapping his finger silently on the tabletop. He's getting agitated and I wonder if Steve is trying to annoy him. Steve has never really forgiven Rogan for taking drugs in the first place back when they were partners; the fallout from that delayed Steve's promotion to sergeant. And then, while Rogan was still an addict, he solved the case of his buddy's murder when we'd ruled it suicide. Then on top of that, after me and Rogan solved the case of that kid's murder, Rogan takes the edge off of Steve's glory by quitting the department to work with me. Yeah, Steve's playing him.

Finally he speaks.

"I can't get a warrant on that."

"What?" we shout in unison. If Steve's playing Rogan, he's taking it too damn far.

"There's a little kid being held captive by a major drug dealer and you can't get—"

"Just hold on a minute there, Cal." Steve is mad. "You can't come in here with a bunch of circumstantial evidence and demand that we start asking the Court for warrants." He stops to take a breath and as Cal opens his mouth Steve stops him with an upheld hand and a face of steel. "Hear me out for once," he continues. "Can't you see the holes in your case? It all seems to revolve around this Razor Point Holdings but you have nothing to tie it to Santiago other than the fact that it owns a car that is used by someone who you think might be linked to Santiago. Hell it could be a car leasing company.

"Plus what have you really got on Perot? I'll tell you what... Nothing. Perot arranges financing for a local production company: well that's his damn job as an MP. He hangs around the set during filming: maybe he just likes the TV business. He's friendly with the families of two girls who go missing: maybe he's friendly with *all* the families. What hard facts have you got?"

"Talk to Radcliffe," Cal says, "he'll tell you."

"Radcliffe would say anything if he thought he could use it to bargain for a lighter sentence." Steve's tone is dismissive.

Steve's right. Although I'm sure Cal is correct, the evidence *is* all circumstantial. We really need something more solid. Maybe if Tyler could confirm that the Shelby is owned by Santiago that would... No. Like Steve said, Razor Point could just be a leasing company.

I look over at Cal. He knows it too. We need to get some solid evidence. Suddenly he stands up. "OK. Just promise me Steve that you'll get your guys looking into this Razor Point Holdings and looking into Perot too."

"I will for sure," Steve says.

Without another word, Cal turns and walks out. I shrug at Steve and wheel after him.

I'm betting he has a plan in mind. Then it hits me.

During the entire time in there, Cal never once mentioned Dave Bradbury, the man behind Razor Point.

44

CAL

The house is beautiful. It's on the waterfront in West Van and, although it's not as impressive as his ex-wife's house, it is beautiful.

The woman who opens the door looks to be in her early twenties and is as stunning as the house. Obviously, Dave Bradbury has wasted none of the short time since he separated from Rebecca. I can feel my anger at him starting to simmer.

"Hello," she says, showing perfect teeth in the perfect smile.

"I'd like to speak to Bradbury. Tell him it's Cal Rogan," The anger ratchets up a few degrees. "I'm investigating the disappearance of his daughter."

"Come in." She opens the door wide and I step through. "Darling, someone's here to see you," she calls. "Come with me." Her smile is genuine and I feel sorry for her.

Bradbury appears from a room to the right of the hallway and his face speeds through a minuscule play. Act one: annoyance. Act two: puzzlement. Act three: fear. He can see my anger.

"What the hell do you think you're doing here?" The fear is in his voice as well.

I leash in the anger. So far it's had a good effect by putting him off balance but I need other skills right now.

I smile. His face starts to relax. He breathes in as a prelude to speech but I pre-empt. "Mr. Bradbury, why were you partying at The Lift on the evening of the day your daughter disappeared?"

The girlfriend walks over and stands beside him.

The question catches him by surprise. "How did you know where I was?"

"Just answer the question, please."

He hesitates. Probably not used to being talked to like this. "Well, I just thought that she was probably playing it up, staying at a friend's house. I had no idea that she was actually missing."

"Come on. She's eight. If it were my daughter, I'd be beside myself."

"It was the sort of thing Ariel might do." He sounds as if even he doesn't believe it.

"OK, supposing I buy that, a couple of nights later you were at the Strathcona School gym for Larry Corliss' town hall meeting and the following Wednesday you were at the debate between Corliss and Perot. On both occasions you looked like a man without a care in the world."

"How do you know what I looked like?" He says aggressively.

"Because I was there. Both times."

"Oh." He looks like a teenager caught in a lie. Then a different thought occurs. "Were you following me, Mr. Rogan. Was that part of your job description as my wife's private detective?"

The girlfriend flushes and walks off down the hallway and into the room Bradbury came out of.

I ignore his question. "So why were you so oblivious to

the fact that your daughter was missing and could have been dead in a ditch at that point?"

"I..." He hesitates again. As he stands there, all the aggression just seems to wash out of him. He looks at me and there is something new in the eyes; he glances over his shoulder at the doorway of the room to which his girlfriend went; it's embarrassment. In little more than a whisper, "I was under a lot of financial pressure at the time and I was in a position where I had to do what a very important client told me. I'm afraid I pushed Ariel's situation out of my mind so that I could do what I needed to do." The way he says it inclines me to believe he's telling the truth. And it fits with what I know.

One itch scratched. But before I scratch the second one, I'm going to need to break him down some more. "That client being Carlos Santiago I assume."

The shock is palpable but he manages to speak over it. "Well... Uh... Yes. Mr. Santiago has a number of legitimate investments which I manage for him."

"Like Razor Point Holdings?"

This time shock overwhelms him. "Wha'... How?" He stops. I can almost hear the wheels clicking in his brain as he tries to respond.

"Razor Point Holdings. The company you control on behalf of Mr. Santiago. The company into which the money you launder for Mr. Santiago is paid. The company that buys cars for his thugs. The company that paid Larry Corliss to abandon his run for the Vancouver East seat. You know, good old Razor Point Holdings."

He opens his mouth and then thinks better of it. The devastation is complete. He doesn't even try to deny it. He stays silent and I can see him trying to weigh options. Now to scratch the second itch, this one I've *got* to know the answer to.

"Why would you invest two hundred thousand dollars of

Mr. Santiago's money in the production of *Canada's Littlest Beauty*? Was it so that Edward Perot could spend time on set grooming the little girls, including your own daughter?"

"What the hell are you talking about? Perot had nothing to do with that investment. Mr. Santiago suggested it to me himself. He'd heard that Ariel was on the show and said it would be a good investment. And it was. He has more than doubled his money in a little less than a year."

I can tell he's telling the truth as far as he knows it. Poor sap doesn't know the real reason Santiago made the investment. Itch scratched.

Now comes the play.

"You realize Mr. Bradbury that when I turn everything I know over to the Organized Crime Section at the VPD, you are going to be facing a charge of laundering the proceeds of crime and probably a slew of others. You're going to be spending several years in jail, not a nice jail at that." I let it sink in. His pallor tells it all: desperation. *To desperation turn my trust and hope.* Ah William, you knew so much.

Time to dangle the bait.

"Do you have a good lawyer?" I ask. A tiny hope glows in the pallor.

"Yes." It's almost like a question.

"I think the police might be very happy to give you amnesty in return for your giving evidence."

I almost feel sorry for him. Fear and hope are fighting the good fight. I watch and wait. I can almost *hear* the battle going on inside his head.

And I wait.

Now the silence is becoming awkward. Good.

And I wait until...

He breaks. "OK. I'll do it."

"Good." If I take charge now, I can get all I want out of this. "Here's what we need to do." *We* not *you*. He's on Team Rogan now. "Get your lawyer to meet us first thing tomorrow morning. It'll be either at VPD's office on Graveley Street or the Crown Prosecutor's office downtown. I'll let you know which within an hour. We'll be meeting with a Sergeant Steve Waters." He nods. "Bring your laptop and bring with you any concrete evidence of Santiago's operations."

He swallows and nods again. "OK."

"You'll need to give all your evidence to them. Your lawyer can negotiate immunity from prosecution with the Crown Prosecutor and the VPD can put you into protective custody while the RCMP organize witness protection for you." I'm totally winging all this. I just need him in the right frame of mind.

He nods, "Good, good."

Now for the last little lie, Kant forgive me. "I'm going to help you with all this and I have some compelling evidence that will make the police more sympathetic to your case. I can't tell you what it is yet, but in return, I will need your help with one little thing."

"Anything, what is it?"

"I am going to arrange a news conference to happen on our way to the police. At that conference, you're going to tell the press that Edward Perot fabricated the evidence that made Larry Corliss withdraw from the election and you're going tell them that Carlos Santiago tried to bribe Corliss on Perot's behalf."

"Why would you care about that?"

"It doesn't matter. My help for you is contingent upon you holding that press conference. Do you understand?"

He thinks for a second then nods.

"Good. Now call your lawyer and have him clear his calendar for tomorrow morning while I organize the VPD."

"I'll do it now." He pulls his phone out of his pocket and as he starts to dial a nasty little worm of suspicion slithers into my mind.

"Wait!" His hand stops, poised over the screen. "How long have you known your lawyer?"

"I don't know, about twelve years."

"Does he also do work for either Perot or Santiago?"

"No."

"You're sure?"

"Yes, absolutely."

"OK, keep dialing." He completes the call and makes arrangements with his lawyer while I plan.

He hangs up. "Ok, he'll be wherever you say and he's going to bring another lawyer from his office who does criminal law. They are going to sit down with me tonight and plan out the details."

"Good. There's one other thing you must do. Don't stay home; go to a hotel and pay cash for the room."

"Why is that?" he asks

"I have to arrange the meeting with the Police and the Crown Prosecutor. When they hear what you have, they will want to arrest you and take control of the situation. They will come straight here to pick you up the moment they hang up the phone with me. It is far better for you to spend the time with your lawyer and meet with them on your terms."

"That makes sense, I'll stay at the—"

"Don't tell me," I interrupt. "When the police ask me where you are I will be able to tell them honestly that I don't know." It's a small salve for my conscience.

"Oh, yes, I see."

Now for the final clincher. "Do you love your daughter Mr. Bradbury?"

He starts at the question. "Of course." He pauses, and realizes. "Oh. I see. Yes, well, over the last few days I haven't been acting like a father who cares, have I?"

I just look at him, feeling disgust at myself at using his feelings for his daughter as a pawn. What would Sam think of me doing that?

"Believe me Mr. Rogan. I do love her very much. Even though I have had to do Santiago's business, Ariel has never been out of my thoughts."

He seems sincere but who can really know another man's heart. "You see, I know where she is."

"Where?" Hope and fear are written equally on his face.

"I believe she is being held at Santiago's estate on Samuel Island. I suspect she is being held there as a reward for Ed Perot."

It takes all of five seconds for the implication to sink in. He has to steady himself by stretching out his hand and propping himself up against the wall. His eyes are wildly searching my face. "They are not your friends Mr. Bradbury. They are using you. We need your evidence so that the police can raid his island and rescue her."

"Perot?" He breathes. "Yes. I can see—" Then it hits him. "I've got to go to the police right now. If Ariel's in danger, we haven't got time to wait. Let me call my lawyer back. We need to see the police right now." He's panicking.

"Don't worry," I tell him, starting to feel sick with my duplicity, "I made a call on my way here and discovered that Perot is in Vancouver at the moment. Ariel is safe from him and you can be sure that Santiago is looking after her. She'll be frightened, yes, but we have to let the police do their job legally, otherwise Santiago and Perot will never be brought to justice and you will be in danger for the rest of your life." The sick feeling has turned to disgust as I say, "I promise she'll be OK. By noon tomorrow she will be back with you."

I pray I'm right. Shakespeare is no comfort now; Cymbeline's prayer rings in my head and will haunt my dreams tonight: *Grant, heavens, that which I fear prove false!*

45

CAL

Although it is poor relief for my battered conscience, Steve has moved fast. He has set up the meeting downtown tomorrow morning with a Crown Prosecutor. He is going to bring his new boss, Inspector Philips, and they are arranging to have a Swat Team ready by the morning to helicopter over to Samuel Island and raid Santiago's estate. He was totally pissed that I didn't tell him about Bradbury earlier but hey, it's the result that counts. Arnold, too, is doing his part and has promised to have a TV news crew and reporters from the *Sun*, *Province* and *Globe and Mail* outside the Prosecutor's office first thing. Steve will be pissed at that too but Bradbury's on-camera exposé is necessary to get Corliss back in the race and Perot out. I owe Corliss at least that much. Arnold, too, for that matter. Doing it this way will produce the best result for all.

Or so I keep telling myself.

Stammo is pleased that I want to help him with Tyler, even when he knows my agenda. We've met with James Garry, the lawyer Stammo has hired for Tyler, and he is with Tyler right now. Stammo and I are just chatting in the lobby waiting; he's in his wheelchair and I'm in a very uncomfortable chair.

Apparently Tyler's dad wasn't happy with how things have gone. Stammo looks the worse for wear. He has turned to his buddies Jim Beam and Jack Daniels quite a bit of late and I don't know whether I should be concerned for him. I feel I should say something but know I'm going to chicken out for now. Instead we take the time to update each other on the other cases that Stammo Rogan Investigations is handling.

A movement to my left catches my eye. It's Garry. He is still wearing his lawyer's collar from court. He comes and sits on an equally uncomfortable seat. He's an older guy with a pleasant, craggily handsome face, a gray beard and long gray hair in a ponytail. Not your typical lawyer. He has a twinkle in his eye that makes him a lot more human than many of his brethren, or is that my jaundiced cop's eye?

He gets straight to the point. "I think we can do something for Tyler. Although he's a low-level member of the gang, he has a *lot* of information about Santiago's operations because of his association with this, uh, Bookman character." He looks at Stammo for a second before continuing. "Combined with the fact that he's got no prior criminal record as an adult, I'm sure I can put together a deal that will avoid his having to do any prison time."

Stammo breathes a very long sigh of relief which earns a wry smile from Garry. His gaze stays on Stammo for a long beat before he continues, "I'll put together a proffer for the CPO and see what we can do."

He stands up and shakes our hands. "You should go and see him now."

"I dunno," says Stammo. "He was pretty pissed with me the last time I saw him."

Garry nods. "I know but he said he wants to talk to you. He's in interview room three. I've told him what he can and can't tell you." He smiles kindly, "He told me you were worried about that."

He walks off toward the doors leading outside.

Stammo looks up at me. "Will you come with me? Please."

"Sure."

He nods and wheels toward the interview rooms. I walk beside him in silence.

A guard checks our visitor badges and lets us into the room. Tyler is sitting at a table. I was expecting teenage anger and resentment but none is present as far as I can see, rather he has an air of deep sadness.

After Stammo makes an awkward introduction of me, he asks, "How y'doing, Ty?"

"Pretty good. The lawyer, Mr. Garry, seems real good."

"He is Ty, he's the best. Whooped me a couple of times in court, I can tell you."

"He told me you're paying for him."

Stammo shrugs.

"Thanks Mr. Stammo, I really appreciate it."

Stammo covers up his emotions with, "He said you wanted to talk to me."

"Yeah... Well... There's something I thought you should know..."

Training kicks in and we both nod, silent and encouraging.

"'Cos after you hear you may not want to pay for... you know, the lawyer an' all."

"What is it Ty?" Stammo says quietly.

"Well my deal, you know, with the lawyers, means I have to give evidence against Mr. Santiago and all his people, including the Bookman."

"Go on." I'm not sure what is happening here but Stammo seems to suspect something... but what? He's biting his lower lip; like smoking, it's another thing he does when he's stressed.

"Well... The Bookman... You know him."

When I first laid eyes on the guy with the snakeskin boots, he looked familiar *and* he knew my name.

"Who the hell is he?" I ask.

Tyler glances at me but then focuses back on Stammo.

"Matt's the Bookman," he says.

Who the hell is Matt?

I look at Stammo. He's as white as a sheet. He leans forward and grabs the desk to steady himself.

Then it clicks.

Matt is Stammo's son.

————

"WE SHOULDN'T BE DOING this Nick. What can you possibly hope to achieve other than to let him know that Tyler has given him up? What if he tells Santiago?" There is no response. "Let's call it a night Nick." He is still silent. He hasn't said more than half a dozen words since Tyler dropped his bombshell. I have to try and deflect him.

He turns his modified van on to Carrall for what must be the hundredth time this evening. We have been cruising a nine-block area surrounding Pigeon Park hoping to see the Shelby.

Finally, "I gotta do it Cal."

The use of my first name doesn't go unnoticed. He only uses it when he's vulnerable.

I nod. "Yeah, I know how you feel but you can't."

"You can go if you want. I could drop you off at your car. But I gotta keep at it. I gotta find out if Tyler was telling the truth and if he was, I gotta talk to him."

I give up. I feel a sudden pull. If he drops me off now, I could go to Pigeon Park and get a baggie of heroin. Just one. Just to take the edge off. Just this once. It'd help me sleep tonight and be ready for the meeting between Dave Bradbury and the Crown Prosecutor. The longing is deep in my gut; it's a real, physical pain.

I turn to him. "OK."

He doesn't look at me but I can see his disappointment. It's a real, physical pain for him too. I push down my longing. It's a hard push. "No, it's OK. I'll stick with you on this."

"Thanks, I appreciate it," he says and goes silent again but this time I know there is more to come. After a while he sighs and the floodgates open, "He was such a bright little kid; he always had his nose in a book. Didn't matter what the subject was, he'd read it. S'probably why they call him the Book-man." He gives a sardonic little chuckle. "He always wanted to do the opposite of what we wanted. If I said something was black, he'd say it was white, y'know?"

"A contrarian," I say.

"Exactly. It was a problem when he got into his teens. Always pushing the limits of the law. Did it 'cos I was a cop eh. I always managed to avoid him getting a record, I'd talk to the arresting officer and get him to look the other way, lose the paperwork."

"Any father would do the same. You can't blame yourself."

"Maybe I should'a done the tough love thing."

We lapse into silence again. My stomach growls.

"Why don't you stop at the Micky D's in International Village. I'll pick us up something."

"Good idea." He signals to go left onto Hastings to loop around to Pender and we both see the Shelby parked right at Pigeon Park. Stammo pulls the van over and parks in front of it. "It wasn't here when we passed by before. What was that, five minutes ago?"

"Yeah," I say. "Listen, we're parked right between the hotel and his car. Why don't I get out, stop him and ask him to come and sit in here with you so you can talk to him."

"Sounds—" His voice is a croak. He clears throat and takes a gulp of the cold coffee in the cup holder on his dash. "Sounds good."

I get out and look back. There is no one in the Shelby. I

scan the faces but don't see any familiar ones; I'm particularly interested in knowing if the muscled thug known as Carl is in evidence but he seems not to be.

I check the area of sidewalk in front of the flophouse: just the usual suspects. I stroll west for a few paces and position myself just past the door and lean against the wall.

"Need a cigarette?"

The seller looks like he's fifteen. I just shake my head; what I need is a hit of heroin. He moves on. "Need a cigarette?" he asks a bag lady pushing a Safeway cart. She ignores him and scurries by. I muse that if he were selling cocaine, which is less addictive than tobacco, he would be breaking the law. As if in tune with my thoughts, through the windshield of Stammo's van, I see a brief glow of red.

The door of the so-called hotel swings open and the Bookman strides out holding a metallic case almost certainly containing a large-ish amount of cash: the day's take. He scans right and left and his face is caught in the light from a streetlamp. I wonder why I didn't see it before: he looks familiar because he is a younger version of his father. But he has a hardness and meanness that Stammo has never had, not even in his worst moments.

I push off the wall and follow him. Just as he draws level with Nick's van I call, "Matt!"

He stops but doesn't immediately turn. I stop maybe three paces behind him, then slowly he pivots and looks at me. "That little twerp Tyler must have squealed," he says. There is a grin on his face; it's cold and cruel and I try not to show the real fear I am feeling. "What do you want Rogan?" I incline my head toward the truck just as the window powers down. He looks and, for the first time in years, locks eyes with his father.

"Hello Matt." Nick's voice is steady now.

I take the three paces and open the passenger door then turn to Matt. "Why don't you get in and have a chat." I say it as nicely as I can but he doesn't move. He stares in and I see a hint of surprise at the sight of Nick's wheelchair.

"What happened to you?" he asks. I cringe at the pleased look on his face which must be knifing into Nick's gut.

"Shit happened." Nick tries to make light of it. "Just get in the car for a moment," he asks. "Please Matt."

Matt holds his father's gaze for a long time. His face is blank but I sense calculations going on in the background. Finally he shrugs, turns to me and hands me the briefcase. "Hold this," he orders then gets into the van, closes the door and powers up the window.

The metal briefcase is heavy. I wonder how much cash is in it. It's a sign of his confidence that he could give it to me without worrying what I might do with it. Arrogant prick. For a moment, I toy with the idea of opening it and handing out the cash to the teeming throng in and around Pigeon Park. It's a delicious thought that I savor like fine wine. But a thought is what it remains; I don't want to upset any agreement that Nick might be able to reach with his son. I'm not hopeful but...

They might be a while.

My stomach growls again. After this we have got to get something to eat. I walk a few paces and sit on a bench facing the van with the briefcase on my lap, like a commuter at a bus stop. I think about tomorrow. When Bradbury tells all to the Crown Prosecutor, they will have the evidence they need to dispatch a S.W.A.T. Team to Samuel Island, Santiago will be under arrest and Ariel will be freed. Poor kid. She's been gone for nine days. I shudder at what she must be going through. I have an almost overwhelming desire to call Ellie, to make sure she's safe and to tell her I love her. Why don't we say those three words to our children every single day? And Sam —I long to call her too. Maybe if Stammo had—

The van door opens and Matt gets out. Without looking back he approaches me, hand held out for the case on my lap.

I stand. It takes all my strength not to drop the case on the sidewalk and make him pick it up but I don't want to jeopardize any accommodation he might have made with Stammo. Not to mention that he frightens me more than I like to admit. I just hand it to him. Six more steps and he is at the Shelby. He opens the door, throws in the case, gets in and peels off down Hastings then turns off onto Cambie and is gone from sight.

Stammo's van smells of smoke. I close the door behind me and crack open the window. "How'd it go?"

"Not good." I look over at him. The masseter muscle in his jaw is pulsing.

"What happened?"

"I tried to get him to see sense. Told him he had to get out before it was too late. That he would go down when Santiago goes down. But he wouldn't listen. Kept telling me that I didn't know what I was talking about. Shit, I pleaded with him but he just wouldn't budge. Stubborn, like his mother." He lapses into silence for a while then, "Let's get that burger."

He guns the engine and pulls into the left-hand lane. As we wait for the light at Abbot, I look left, just in time to see a single tear trickle down his cheek.

I look away.

While I'm waiting for those burgers, I am definitely going to call Sam and Ellie and tell them both that I love them.

46

CAL

MONDAY

S teve and I are standing with Hank King from the Crown Prosecutor's office. I worked with King on the last case Stammo and I had as cops. He has a hawk face and a mind like a steel trap; defendants and their witnesses, and sometimes even their attorneys, will often break under his sharp gaze. He and Steve are talking tactics, leaving me to worry. What if Bradbury doesn't show; maybe I misread him. Maybe he's taken the time since I met with him yesterday to fly off to some sunny haven without an extradition agreement with Canada. A worse thought swoops in from nowhere: what if he's chickened out and told Santiago in exchange for Ariel.

Either of those scenarios would be my fault for not taking him in to the VPD last night. I justified my decision based on needing to give Arnold time to organize news coverage on behalf of Larry Corliss. Now I'm doubting my own wisdom. Wisdom? I remember a philosophy professor whom I greatly admired saying, *Wisdom is a level of understanding that as soon as you think you have some, the Universe proves to you that you don't.* I hope that's not prophetic.

I wish Stammo were here. Funny, I wouldn't have thought

those words a year or so ago but on our last case as cops and on our cases since, I have come to value his good points and to truly value our partnership. I don't want to think about what he's going through right now. I feel like I should have called him this morning just to check in on him. Maybe later.

I look around to distract myself.

A flash of color to my right draws my attention to a bright green Lamborghini growling its way down Hornby. It passes a parked Rolls Royce. One that I know. One that I have sat in only once. I can just see Arnold through the windshield. I wave. He doesn't. Just a slight bob of his head acknowledges me.

For about the tenth time, I check my watch. Eight thirty-eight. Bradbury's late.

I look at the newspeople. A gaffer with a microphone in its covering—which always reminds me of the bearskin cap of one of those English soldiers who silently guards Buckingham Palace—nudges the cameraman and points at the retreating Lambo. A reporter holding a second mic is on her cell but is not talking into it. She is staring across the street at the Law Courts building with its vast sloping glass roof. Suddenly she turns and looks north on Hornby; the person on the phone must have given her a heads-up. I follow her gaze and see three men striding along the sidewalk toward us. In the center is Dave Bradbury, flanked by two suits who must be his lawyers. One of them is pulling a suitcase on wheels which I'm guessing, and hoping, holds Bradbury's files and laptop. I breathe a huge sigh of relief.

The reporter has galvanized her troops into action and is making a line for the approaching trio. One of Bradbury's lawyers steps forward and holds up a hand indicating they should stop and says something to them that I can't quite hear. Bradbury has stopped in his tracks, looking nervous. I hope he doesn't chicken out in front of the camera. The other lawyer, the one closest to the curb, takes a step back. Not like any defense lawyer I've ever met. They usually love to hog a camera, taking any opportunity they can to advocate for their client—and for themselves, my cynical side says.

I forget all that and listen to the first lawyer. "My client, Mr. David Bradbury, has a statement to make prior to meeting with the authorities."

He steps back a half pace and the other lawyer takes another two steps backward. Odd. Bradbury steps forward toward the reporter. He looks uncertain. I would too. He is about to break with the people who have made him a very rich man over the last few years, people who will make him a very marked man for the rest of his years. He looks over and catches my eye. I smile encouragement to him. He takes a deep breath and takes a second step closer to the microphone which the gaffer is dangling a few inches above his head.

Bradbury stumbles and a puzzled look crosses his face. He looks down as I hear an unmistakable crack. I glance at Steve, he has heard it and is reaching for his weapon. Bradbury crumples to the ground and I hear a second crack. The news crew is looking down at the body and I scan the buildings behind the Law Courts looking for any telltale sign of the shooter. A third crack and Bradbury's lawyer drops to the ground. I can hear the hubbub but snap my attention back on the buildings, looking desperately for anything unusual. Nothing. I glance back at Bradbury trying to estimate trajectories. Everyone, including the second lawyer, is backing away from the fallen bodies except for the cameraman who is focusing in on the shot that will make his career. Only Hank King runs forward to attempt first aid. I cut a quick glance at Steve. He's focused on a building about two hundred yards away on the other side of the Law Courts.

He points. "I think I saw something on the roof there." He says. He holsters his gun and pulls out his cell.

A shooter on a roof has to come down to escape. Without thought I dash across Hornby and down Smithe. I am calculating. The building that Steve pointed to is about twelve floors. It would take the shooter about twenty seconds to clear the roof; he won't want to take an elevator, it's too confining. He is probably dashing down the stairs as I run under the section of the Law Courts that is like a bridge over Smithe. Say he can make five or six seconds per flight of stairs, it will take him about a minute and a quarter to reach ground level. Just enough time. Maybe.

As I hit Howe, the traffic is light enough that I can dash across. I make a beeline for the lobby of the building acutely aware that I'm not as fit as I used to be. The sign over the door says Robson Court. I push through the doors. As I stand panting, I take in the scene. A couple of people are standing waiting for elevators. Dressed in business casual, they look like they belong. To the right of the elevators is a door that looks like it leads to a stairwell. I head toward it and redo my calculation. He will come through any second. An elevator pings. No one walks out. The people in the lobby get in. As the doors close a second elevator pings. This time a man gets out. Looks about sixty, a hundred pounds overweight, carrying a tiny briefcase that wouldn't hide a disassembled long gun.

I open the door to the stairs and listen. A door slams and then silence. Damn! He's left through the back entrance. I run through the stairwell and down a couple of steps. There is a steel door with a crash bar in front of me. I push it open and find myself in the loading bay at the back of the building. No sign of the shooter. I jump down into the area where the trucks back into the loading dock and run to the alley. Nothing to the right. To the left about fifty yards down a man is throwing something into the back seat of a nondescript black car that looks about twenty years old; a light mist of exhaust is bubbling from the tailpipe. He slams the back door and glances back as he opens the front passenger door. Our eyes meet. Instant recognition. I go into a sprint. He hesitates a second—he's thinking 'fight or run'—then decides and hops into the car which takes off in a squeal of tires before he has even closed the passenger door, allowing me to see a brief flash of snakeskin boot.

———

STEVE HAS the good grace not to excoriate me for my lack of wisdom in not bringing Dave Bradbury in last night. He doesn't have to: I can't get the words of King Lear's Goneril out of my mind: *You are much more at task for want of wisdom.* Bradbury may have made a great deal of money laundering Santiago's funds but he didn't deserve to die for it, especially as he was just about to redeem himself. My decision has made his daughter fatherless.

Despite Hank King's pleas, Bradbury's secondary lawyer has refused to release the laptop and documents that Bradbury was bringing to us, claiming that the documents are now the property of his wife and she will need to give her permission for their release. I have another suspicion. Did this lawyer stand back from his client because he knew what was going to happen to Bradbury and his main lawyer? Something to get Steve to look into at some point in the future. But right now, saving Ariel is the priority.

Hank has listened to the details of my investigation and asked some probing questions but says it just isn't enough to get a warrant for Santiago's property, unless there is something in Bradbury's files. It all hangs on Rebecca Bradbury giving her permission for those files to be released to the Crown Prosecutor's office.

She surely will when she knows they are the key to getting a warrant that will allow us to free Ariel. There's just one catch.

Despite attempts by the VPD, nobody seems to know where Rebecca Bradbury is.

47

STAMMO

ow are you doing?" He asks. I can read it all in his face. What he's really asking is if I drank myself to sleep last night. He can see the redness in my eyes but I'm not about to tell him about how it got there.

"I'm just aces." I couldn't keep the sarcasm out of my voice. "Sorry." He nods and gives a half smile. Uh-oh. "How'd it go with Bradbury?" I ask.

"It didn't. He got shot."

I feel the blood drain out of my face. Trying to keep my face straight and voice steady I ask him, "Who shot him?" But I ask myself, *My God, what have I done?* When I talked to Matt I told him he should leave Santiago's gang, that Santiago was about to go down. Did they guess that Bradbury was the weak link? Am I the one responsible for his death?

"I dunno," he says. I feel a wave of relief except… there's a look on his face.

"You sure?"

"Well, it was obviously someone on Santiago's payroll; it could have been anyone."

"But it wasn't just anyone was it Rogan?" He looks at me. He doesn't want to say it. So I do. "It was Matt wasn't it?" He nods. "Is he under arrest?" He shakes his head and I feel another wave of relief. "But the cops know it was him?"

"Kinda," he says.

"What'ja mean, kinda?"

"I saw him escaping. I had to tell Steve but I told him it was the Bookman. I didn't mention that he was your kid."

I feel more relief than I should. "Thanks Cal."

"S'OK." He smiles.

We sit silent for a moment. We both know that the Bookman's identity will be known by all soon enough.

"So what happens now?," I ask.

"Bradbury brought all the evidence we need to get a warrant on Santiago but after he was shot, his damn lawyer wouldn't release it to us without Rebecca's permission and she seems to have gone missing." He checks his watch. "They've been trying to track her down for the last couple of hours but there's nothing. Steve said he'd call me as soon as he heard from her."

"What if the worst has happened? What if Santiago has had her killed or maybe Bradbury was after the last of her money and had it done."

We both mull that over. I can't help thinking about that poor little kid, Ariel. What she must be going through now plus what will happen when she's rescued only to find out her father's dead and her mother... Where the hell is Rebecca Bradbury? Shit. We gotta *do* something. And Matt. Last time I talked to the guys in the drug squad, they didn't know who the Bookman was, didn't have a photo or nothing. Maybe Matt'll be in the clear. That fuckin' Santiago. Turning kids like Matt and Tyler into criminals, murderers.

"Fuck Santiago." I say it out loud.

"I hear you," Rogan says. "Anyone who kidnaps a little kid to keep a pedophile MP on his payroll doesn't deserve to draw breath."

"Yeah, but without good, solid evidence there's nothing

we can do. We can't tie Bradbury to Santiago and we can't tie Perot to him either."

Rogan looks at his watch and grabs the remote control for the little TV we keep in the office. "Let's see what CBC's got to say about the Bradbury killing."

Just as it comes on they are showing the footage of Bradbury's lawyer. He's saying, *"...has a statement to make prior to meeting with the authorities."* Bradbury takes a step forward, looks at something, then stumbles and falls. The camera shakes for a moment, then focuses on him lying on the sidewalk, then there is a cut to the News anchor. *"We won't show the balance of the footage as it may upset younger or more sensitive viewers. Mr. Bradbury was a successful local entrepreneur who was also a supporter of East Vancouver MP, Edward Perot, who had this to say..."* The scene switches to an interview with Perot.

Fuck. It's him.

"That's Perot?" I shout.

"Yeah, why?" he says without taking his eyes from the screen.

"I've seen him before. In the Bookm— in Matt's car. That's the proof we need."

No reaction. He just keeps staring. As Perot speaks, I can hear a growling in Rogan's throat. He looks like he's going to throw something at the TV. Perot is doing the typical politician thing whenever there's a high profile murder. He's yammering on about law and order. All fucking talk. Nothing ever happens. Perot finishes with, *"I will be on the Gulf Islands on Wednesday and will be flying to Ottawa Thursday night. I have arranged a meeting on Friday morning with the Prime Minister to finalize the details of the new anti-drug bill which I will introduce into the House with his full support—"*

Rogan stabs the remote at the screen and it goes blank. "You know what that means." He's on his feet raging now. "It means he's going to Santiago's island for his reward. The reward for turning around the government's stance of legalization. And you know what that reward is: it's poor little Ariel. There's gotta be a way to stop him."

I want to stand up and rage with him. Damn this wheelchair! "There's nothing we can do," I say. "Without solid evidence, Santiago's golden." Wait a minute. "Wait. What about this. I can tie Perot to Santiago. I saw him in the Shelby."

He turns it over in his mind then shakes his head. "Yeah, but without Bradbury's evidence about Razor Point Holdings we can't tie the car to Santiago. It's all the proof *we* need but it's not evidence."

We look at each other, at a loss for words.

His anger deflates and I see a new look on his face. A look I've seen before. That's his I-have-an-idea look. Then it hits. "Are you thinking what I think you're thinking?" I ask.

He slowly nods.

48

CAL

W hy do I have to go to Mommy's house? I'm supposed to get tonight *and* tomorrow night with you this week." Ellie stamps her foot to emphasize her frustration. It is a funny image and I have to suppress the desire to smile.

"It's because of Ariel sweetie," I say. "You know I'm trying to help find her and bring her back to her Mommy and Daddy." She nods but is not yet completely mollified. "Well, tonight I have to meet with Mr. Stammo and we are going to do some things that will help to rescue her."

"Oh OK." She gives me a big smile. "I hope you find her Daddy."

"I do too." I reach down and hug her. "Get your backpack, put your coat on and we'll go over to Mommy's."

As she bustles about getting her stuff together, I think again about the enormity of the task that Stammo and I have to prepare for. We planned it out in detail this afternoon and we have just thirty-two hours left to complete the preparations. I run through the checklist in my head; it helps me focus on the task and not think too much about the consequences.

She's ready quickly and we step out through the front door. As I lock it behind us, I have a frisson of fear. Will I still be alive to unlock it on Saturday morning?

We go to the garage in silence and get into the car.

As she clicks her seatbelt in place, she says, "Locked and loaded and ready to rumble." It's our code.

"Let's do it," I reply and fire up the Healey's engine.

As I pull out of the garage she says, "Daddy, I'm glad I told you I want to be a policeman like you. Mommy said it was OK to tell you too."

I feel a stirring of pride. "That's good sweetie," I say, "but you know I'm not a policeman anymore." One day I will tell her the story of why I left the VPD, then rejoined and then left again in order to start up with Stammo.

"I know but you still are *kind* of a policeman, right?"

"Kind of," I agree.

"So you do good things to help people?"

"Sometimes I do bad things to help people." That slipped right out. I definitely didn't mean to say that.

She's silent for a while. Good. Maybe she didn't catch it. Then, "So it's OK to do a bad thing if it helps someone?"

"Well, I, uh…" Best to draw the moral straight line. "No. No sweetie, it's not right to do a bad thing to achieve a good thing."

"But you said you do bad things to help people."

"I know I did… but I was wrong."

She goes silent again and leaves me to struggle with the fact that I am about to do a very bad thing to achieve a good thing. I rationalize the hell out of it but still can't shake the knowledge that I don't have a moral leg to stand on. What we are about to do will save Ariel but… And what if Ariel is already dead? It will have been for nothing.

I continue my internal struggle until we get to Sam's condo.

I lock the Healey, hoping that it will be OK on the street

for the next couple of nights, and we walk hand-in-hand up the steps to the front door.

She welcomes us in with a big smile, hugs Ellie and kisses me on the cheek, which sends a little tingle down my spine. "Thanks for taking her Sam. I have to go away with Stammo for a couple of days. It's the Ariel Bradbury case."

"My pleasure." She takes my arm and leads me toward the kitchen. The gentle pressure of her breast against my arm combines with the smell of her perfume and creates a strong reaction in my body. She squeezes tighter. "Elles Bells," she calls, "Go upstairs, there's a bath ready for you, no need to wash your hair, just a quick bath, jammies on, then call us and we'll come upstairs and tuck you in."

"OK Mommy." She runs upstairs making slightly less noise than a herd of elephants might.

Sam takes me into the kitchen. There are two glasses of wine on the granite countertop. But instead of walking over to them, she pushes the kitchen door closed and puts her arms around my neck. She presses her body toward me and, feeling the growing pressure, she smiles and gently grinds her pelvis against mine. As I incline my head toward hers, the smile fades away and her lips open slightly.

I have been dreaming of this moment for over six years. I can feel my heartbeat. Our lips touch gently at first then part and then come together again with a rising passion. The tips of our tongues flicker together and I hug her closer. The kiss is long and deep. As we break away to breathe, she kisses the side of my mouth, then my cheek and then whispers in my ear so closely that the heat of her breath sets my whole body vibrating. "Stay the night." Oh yes, yes, yes. Six years of longing are finally over.

"Sam, I love you."

"I love you too."

We kiss again. She slides her right hand down from behind my neck and slips it between us. As she touches me, I want to explode. I glide my hands under her sweater, onto her naked skin.

A car horn sounds on the street outside.

I move my hand up and cup her naked breast. "Mmmm," she purrs as I—

The car horn sounds again. Three deliberate blasts. Stammo. He said he would pick me up at eight.

"Sam, I have to go. That honking is Stammo. We have to leave now."

Her disappointment is written all over her face. "Really, Cal? Really?" She pulls away but not completely.

"I'm so sorry Sam." I realize I am still holding her breast. I let it go feeling stupid. She looks at my stricken face and giggles.

"It'll keep," she says and kisses me quickly on the lips. "When will you be back?"

"Saturday."

"Well, California Rogan, on Saturday night I am going to…" she leans forward and whispers the rest of the sentence. I don't know if it was so Ellie wouldn't hear the words, or if it was to set my body tingling anew from the hot breath in my ear.

Stammo's horn blasts again and I wonder if I will be back here whole in mind and body on Saturday night.

49

CAL

Thinking of Sam and of Ellie and of being a family again has helped me through the last forty-eight hours. Last night I got about five hours sleep deep in the woods in my newly acquired bivvy bag, but it is the only sleep I have had since I walked regretfully away from Sam's front door. After a day of watching, my head is starting to nod. I check my watch; it's Wednesday at seven-thirty and the sun is heading off across the Pacific, casting shadows of the trees I have been hiding in for the last thirteen hours, across from the immaculate lawns of Carlos Santiago's Samuel Island estate.

Maybe Edward Perot's not going to show. Maybe Carlos Santiago isn't even here; I've certainly seen no sign of him in the over twelve hours I've been watching. I wonder for the thousandth time if we have got this all wrong and Ariel isn't here at all. The rage I felt on Monday, when Stammo and I hatched this plan, has subsided and I'm wondering if I can go through with it without that rage to spur me on.

Also for the thousandth time I scan the scene before me with my binoculars. Off to the far left is the beach with the dock and the long, low boat that I saw on Salt Spring Island carrying the phony cop Sherri Oliver away. I look out to sea and can see no sign of any boat inbound to the island carrying Edward Perot to his weekend getaway.

To the far right is the imposing mansion, its pristine white tinted rose by the soon-to-be setting sun. Beside it, about two hundred yards from me is what I assume to be quarters for the estate's guards, I have watched their comings and goings all day. To my horror, I have observed eight of them. All dressed in fatigues, all sporting stubbly beards and all bearing AK-47s. Two are sitting on stools outside the main house. Clearly, Carlos Santiago feels under threat and clearly his guards make my task doubly hard and my escape many times more so. Behind the guards' HQ are the kennels housing an unknown number of dogs. I can see only three but at times can hear more. The most fearsome is a monster who looks like a cross between a Pit Bull and a Rottweiler, chestnut brown with a white patch over his left eye.

Apart from the movements of the guards there has been absolutely no activity on the estate for the whole day.

I put the binocs down and check my watch again. Five minutes later than the last time I looked. I'm probably going to have to spend tonight in the forest behind me. I check my stuff, also for the thousandth time. My backpack is bulging with my camping gear and emergency supplies. The bivvy bag is rolled and strapped to the backpack. I have my binocs slung around my neck and attached to my belt is a water bottle and the hunting knife Stammo insisted I take. "Can't go camping without one," he insisted. I have to say he has been great. He was a Boy Scout leader when Matt was a kid and what he doesn't know about camping and survival isn't worth knowing. That plus his military background are the only things that have made this job possible.

I check the last item. It's a Winchester Model 70, built in 2012 by FN Herstal so Stammo tells me. It's not the absolute best rifle for the job but at this range it should be enough. My only experience shooting a rifle was with the Army Cadets when I was at school. I was pretty good then and during our practice yesterday, I was consistently able to hit targets at three hundred yards. It's enough distance for today but will it be different when the targets are breathing and not just paper?

As I worry the thought, I see movement in front of the house. A woman has come out through the main door, beside her is a girl.

My trembling fingers can hardly steady the binoculars. I adjust the focus and right there I am looking at the face of Ariel Bradbury. "Thank God," I breathe. She is wearing a frilly, lacy skirt with white stockings and black patent leather shoes. Her top is red and sequined and her hair looks like it has been curled. She is every bit *Canada's Little Beauty*. Santiago's people have dressed her up like this for the pleasure of Edward Perot. I can feel the rage returning. Good. Very good.

I watch as they walk about the lawn. The woman beside her is dressed in a maid's uniform—I'd thought they went out of fashion in the last century—she is talking to Ariel and smiling. What kind of woman—? Maybe she doesn't know what is planned for her.

Maybe if I could take a photo and email it to Steve, it would be good enough evidence for a warrant. I won't have to use the Winchester.

I fumble my phone out of my pocket.

They get close to the beach and Ariel points to it, looking up at her minder. The woman shakes her head. I train the phone on them. They are a long way away. I wonder if my phone's got a good enough resolution to confirm who it is. I take one picture. Not too good, Ariel is mostly turned away from me.

A voice shouts something in Spanish; the guards are on their feet. One of them is pointing out to sea. The huge dog gives a couple of barks.

The maid hurries Ariel back to the house. I snap off a couple of photos but the maid is now between Ariel and me. I keep taking them until they disappear inside. I quickly check the pix. No good. Then I notice there are no bars on my phone. I can't send them anyway. Damn!

Then I hear it. The unmistakable *woomp-woomp-woomp* of helicopter blades. My heart starts racing in tempo. A helicopter. I had expected them to arrive by boat.

Anyway it is now, as they say, show time.

I remove the binocs and put them and my water bottle and a half-finished sandwich into the backpack and zip it closed. I do a last check of the ground. I have left nothing. I take the Winchester and walk two trees to my left. The tree is an Arbutus; it's one of the reasons I chose this spot. Not for its beauty but because the trunk conveniently splits into two at chest height. I lean into the trunk and settle my left triceps in the crook between the boughs. I nestle the stock of the Winchester into my right shoulder and force myself to breathe steadily.

The helicopter has to land on the lawn, the forest is too close to the back of the house to provide a safe landing spot. I'm guessing and hoping that it will land as far away from the house as possible, which should place it nearer to me. I adjust the sight for a range of one hundred and fifty meters. I look up at the helo, it's less than half a mile away. Then it hits me. The pilot could be used to track me. What with the speedboat, the armed guards, the dogs and now the helo, my chances of a clean escape are dwindling toward zero.

The helicopter is close now. It seems almost overhead. It is shiny black and carries no markings other than the registration letters. Its body rotates so that it is facing the mansion and it floats down to the corner of the lawn closest to me. I whisper a quiet thank you to Mars, the god of war. Then a curse. The passenger door is on the side facing away from me. The helicopter will shield whoever gets out. Assuming they walk straight to the door of the mansion they will come into view about halfway across the lawn.

If I were to move about a hundred yards to the right, I would have a better shooting angle. But I don't have time. The guards are now looking in this general direction so they might see me. I adjust the scope for the extra distance.

The helicopter touches down and the engine pitch drops. I see movement through the window and it looks like the passengers are starting to debark. The first person I see is Stammo's son. He walks briskly to a position about twenty yards to the front of the helicopter. He stops, looks back and gives a brief wave to the pilot. He looks over toward the beach area for a second and then turns back and scans the forest. For a second he is looking straight toward me. It's not possible that he can see me is it? I find I am holding my breath but he turns around and heads briskly over to the guards' quarters.

I return to steady breathing in rhythm with the helicopter's slowing blades. I scrunch down to shooting position and remember the plan. If it's only one of them, take him out. If it's both, take Santiago first because Perot is less likely to realize what's happening and take evasive action.

Ten seconds and I see Santiago. He's walking toward the house with Perot striding beside him in lockstep. The perfect metaphor for the collusion between politics and drugs.

I sight the crosshairs, breathe, hold, squeeze one, squeeze two and the Winchester pounds against my shoulder. Bolt up, back, forward, down. Site the crosshairs on Perot—he is standing over Santiago probably asking him if he's OK—breathe, hold, squeeze one, squeeze two.

I survey my handiwork and tap the headset. "Both down."

"Good man. I'll make the call. Get out of there fast."

One thing first. Bolt up, back, forward, down. I take aim at the helo's rotor mechanism and fire the third bullet. I see a piece of metal fly off and hear the clang of the bullet a small fraction of a second later.

I scoop up the two spent cases, fumble to unzip the backpack, drop them in and re-zip. Note to self: should have left it unzipped. Both guards are running toward the fallen figures. The Winchester goes in its case and my hands tremble as I try to fasten it to the backpack. A quick glance and I see two more guards spilling out of the guardhouse. One looks toward the dock and the other scans the forest but I'm pretty sure that he can't see me through the trees.

I finally fasten the gun case to the carabiners on the backpack; thirty precious seconds spent. I stand and do a last scan of the ground. I can't see any sign of my sojourn here. I take one last look at the scene. I hear a voice shout, "Son muertos!" They're dead. I feel the first twinge of regret that I know will follow me for the rest of my life but I can console myself with the fact that Ariel is now safe and there is one pedophile and one drug lord fewer in the world. Three more guards are in evidence and two of them are heading toward the kennels. It's time to go.

I slip my left arm in the backpack's strap and something punches me in my right side. I stumble but don't go down. I turn. He is standing there with what looks like a Sig Sauer in his left hand. I look down. A bloom of red is soaking through my clothing.

"We meet again, Rogan. Third time's a charm." Matt Stammo, the Bookman, has a big smile on his face.

50

STAMMO

S teve. Listen. Rogan and I are on a boat just off Samuel Island. We've been putting Santiago's property under surveillance."

"Uh-huh." Well at least he's listening.

"Anyways, we just heard some shooting. Exigent circumstances eh?"

He's silent for a bit. *"Could be someone hunting or doing target practice."*

I gotta improvise here. "What, with machine guns?"

"Machine guns?" That little white lie got his attention.

"Yeah. Three or four of them. Sounds like a war's going on." Silent again. "It's your chance to get in there and save that little kid." Still silent. "And maybe grab Santiago too."

"You better be right about this Nick. I'll call you back and let you know what's happening." He hangs up.

I put on my headset and thumb the button. "I think Steve's going for it. Get to the rendezvous ASAP."

No reply.

"You there Cal?"

Silence.

He must be running and doesn't want to talk.

"Cal?"

"Hello Daddy dearest."

51

CAL

He just stands there. Gun in hand and a cruel smile on his face. I now know why I never made the connection to Stammo. Although their faces are similar, Stammo could never muster the menace and cruelty coming in waves off his son.

My right hand is applying pressure to the wound but blood is seeping through my fingers. This is not good. The only saving grace is that Matt has shown himself to be a rank amateur. I should be dead. Twice. He only wounded me with his first shot and he hasn't finished me off with a second one.

"I think Steve's going for it. Get to the rendezvous ASAP," says Stammo's voice in my headset. I can't tap it to answer. My left hand is raised and my right is on the wound.

Matt's head cocks to one side; he heard the sound of the headset.

He saunters over to where I am standing and rips the headset off me.

"You there Cal?" Matt's grin broadens. He examines the device.

"Cal?"

Matt taps the Send button. "Hello Daddy dearest," he says.

There is silence from Nick.

"Fuck you." Matt throws the headset on the ground and grinds the heel of his snakeskin boot into it, giving me my only chance. In his eagerness to spurn his father, he has come too close to me and has let the gun waver away from my direction. My left hand comes down and chops his wrist right on the scaphoid. The Sig discharges and drops to the ground. He makes another rookie mistake and bends to pick it up only to get kicked in the face by my boot. It hasn't got a lot of force behind it but it makes him roll away from the gun. I don't repeat his mistake but am able to kick the gun away from him.

I take a step forward but he is on his feet fast. I aim a jab at his nose but he weaves to his left and jabs a fist into my wound. I grunt at the pain and feel a flush of warmth from fresh blood flowing out of it. I take an unexpected step toward him and nail him with a straight right to the nose. It was a good solid punch and he is temporarily blinded. Now's my chance. I make for the gun but my toe catches on a tree root which over the years has pushed its way up from below. I crash to the ground and there is an excruciating pain from the wound. I yell out.

As I struggle to my feet he is on me. He knocks me back down and is straddled across my thighs. He punches down into the wound and as my stomach muscles tense my head comes forward only to receive a second punch. I see stars and there is a roaring in my head. I'm done for if he does that again.

But he's an amateur; he doesn't push home his advantage. He looks at me with a sneer written across his face and says, "Do you know what, Rogan?" I'll never know what he was going to tell me. My right hand rips Stammo's hunting knife from its scabbard and without thought plunges it under his rib cage.

His eyes go wide. He tries to speak but it just comes out as a gurgle. He falls forward on top of me.

I push off his dead weight and get to my feet.

I look toward the estate. One of the guards standing by the unmoving bodies is on a cell phone. The woman who walked Ariel on the lawn just a few minutes ago is running toward them. Of more concern are the two guards who were running toward the kennels; they now have two of the dogs on leashes and are pointing in my general direction alerted by the sound of Matt's gun.

I open the backpack and pull out the duct tape that Stammo made me pack. *Never go anywhere without duct tape,* he said. I use my teeth to tear off a long strip of it, pull up my sweater and grimace at the exit wound. I feel around my side and find where the bullet entered my flesh and slap one end of the duct tape on it, the other end I wind round my side and cover most of the exit wound. I have to get moving now. The dogs and their minders are no more than two hundred yards away. Once they decide to move…

One last thing…

I turn to Matt's lifeless body and pull the hunting knife bearing my bloody fingerprints out of him. I drop it in the backpack, zip it up and throw it onto my shoulders. Without a look back, I run along the path into the forest. Behind me I can hear the baying of the dogs. They are coming. And when they smell the blood…

52

STAMMO

I t's been fifteen minutes since the last transmission: two words from Matt that just about broke my heart. The whole plan's fucked up. Santiago and Perot may be dead but Matt has taken Rogan and thanks to me the VPD SWAT team are on their way to the island. The first thing they're gonna do is arrest Matt, and Rogan too. They'll be coming after me soon enough as an accessory. What were we thinking?

I don't know what to do now. Here I am on my old army buddy's Sea Ray bobbing up and down a mile off of Samuel Island with the running lights off. I suppose I'd better head back to his mooring on Pender and wait for—

Explosions! The pipe bombs. Someone's tripped the booby trap. That doesn't make sense. Unless… Unless Rogan's escaped. That's it! Maybe he talked Matt around and they're escaping together. Or maybe the pipe bombs…? No, I can't think that. I got to assume the plan's still on. The next thing should be the decoy boat.

Come on Cal. Come on Matt. It shouldn't be long now. Not more than a couple of minutes.

The waiting is killing me.

There's a burst of gunfire. What does that mean? As I strain my eyes to see any sign of movement, I see running lights. I grab the binocs and focus on them. It's the cigarette boat. I can hear the engines now. If they're patrolling the island, it must mean that Rogan and Matt have escaped. The boat's moving fast about a hundred yards out from the shoreline I'm guessing. It passes between me and the bay where—The flashing beacon! I can see it now. The decoy boat with the mannequin at its helm. They *must* be OK.

The cigarette boat is turning toward the dinghy. I grab my cell phone. Just give it a moment. I see muzzle flashes followed by the sound a second later. Perfect. They're firing at it. I hit the preset number on the phone and wait while the phone dials. A second round of muzzle flashes coincides with the explosion. Perfect. The bottom of the dinghy blows out and takes all the evidence to the bottom of the Strait of Georgia, leaving the gang believing they got the assassin.

Now I have to wait until the cavalry arrives. Then I can go in and pick up Matt and Rogan when all the hubbub has died down.

Maybe I'll be able to make things OK with Matt. He must have learned his lesson from this. With Santiago dead he's got no reason to stay on in the gang. I'm pretty sure I can turn him around. Be like a family again.

53

CAL

THURSDAY

I t's four AM and the cold is really getting to me now. The heating units in the modified dry suit have all stopped working. The batteries lasted longer than I expected but with my clothing wet, the cold has really set in. All activity on the beach seems to have stopped. A couple of hours ago there were men with flashlights who I suppose were members of the SWAT team scouring the island for the assassin but I doubt they'll be back before dawn.

I'll just hang in here.

I can't wait to get back to see Sam and Ellie. Just the thought of them is somehow healing. They must never know what I've done here. The ends may seem to justify the means but I know in my heart that I have committed cold-bloodied murder—both a crime and a moral abomination.

And how do I tell Stammo about Matt? That I killed him with the knife Stammo gave me.

A throbbing reaches me through the waters. Equal parts of relief and dread flood through me. The sound resolves itself. Boat engine. Two of them creating a pulsing through the water. He's close. I undo the weight belt.

Pain lances through me as I stand. In the moonlight I can

just make out Stammo in his buddy's Sea Ray. I wave and wade forward, he waves back and skillfully rotates the boat so that I can clamber onto the swim grid at the back. It's painful but I make it.

I go forward and sit on the seat beside him. The grin on his face fades. "Where's Matt?" Oh God, it's worse than I thought. He thinks Matt escaped with me.

"He didn't make it Nick," the words trip off my tongue. "I'm really sorry."

He goes silent for a moment, then moves the gears into forward and powers the boat away from the shore. He stays silent until we clear the bay and are in open water en route to Pender. Finally he says, "How?"

"He tried to stop me."

"You mean Santiago and Perot are still alive?" He shouts his anger.

"No, no I got them both. He tried to stop me escaping."

He turns to me, his face a mask of fury. "So you killed him?! My son tried to stop you escaping so you fucking killed him!"

"He shot me. He was going to finish me off. I had no choice. I'm sorry Nick, it was him or me."

"HE WAS MY SON!"

"I know, I'm sorry."

"YOU KILLED MY SON!"

He throttles back and the nose of the boat dips. It slows then comes to a stop and bobs on the water, the scream of the engines now a quiet burble.

"Nooooooo—" His howl of rage is cut off by wracking sobs. "He... was... my son." The words spill out between sobs. "My... son."

I have no words. No Shakespeare. Nothing comes to soothe his anguish. No words will help.

I pull myself to my feet and kneel beside him. Tentatively I put an arm around his shoulder. He tenses for a moment and then sags forward, his face to my chest. I hold him like a child until the sobbing stops, repeating, "I'm sorry Nick. I am so sorry." Tears are streaming down my face now.

Finally, after an age, he takes a deep breath and exhales a broken sigh. "It wasn't your fault. If anything it was mine. If I'd been a better father..." He leaves the words hanging.

"You can't blame yourself. Matt probably couldn't help what he'd become. It's just life."

He straightens up and pulls back his shoulders so that my arm drops away. "It's just life." He tries out the words but his voice says they are not enough.

"I guess we'd better go." He sounds unsure and just sits there at the helm.

I stand up and pain lances through me. I grunt.

Easing myself into the seat beside me I say, "Nick, I was shot, it's pretty bad. I'm going to need first aid."

The words give him a reason for action. "Why didn't you say that for Chris'sake." He pushes the levers forward and the boat accelerates hard. "My buddy who lent me the boat was a medic in the Gulf War. He's seen more bullet wounds than you can imagine. He'll fix you up, no questions asked. We'll be there soon enough. You go below and lie down and I'll call ahead." I stay sitting beside him while he makes the call. When he's finished he reiterates his suggestion that I go and lie down but I don't.

I stare ahead at the lights of Pender Island pondering the enormity of what I have done.

54

SAM

SUNDAY

W hat a strange dream. I stretch and roll on my back. I start before I remember that the man lying beside me is Cal. Ah, yes. I snuggle up to him feeling the beautiful sensation of naked flesh on naked flesh. He stirs in his sleep but doesn't wake; he said that he hasn't had much sleep over the last few days. I put my arm across his chest and feel the roughness of the bandage running round his stomach. He didn't want to talk about it; said it was a minor scrape, not more than a scratch, but I don't really believe that.

I think the case that he and Nick have just concluded has taken a lot out of him. He wouldn't speak about it other than to say that Ariel Bradbury was rescued but that her father was dead. But I know there was a lot more to it than that. A couple of times last night I saw a great melancholy descend on him. Although it gave me the chance to hug him and kiss him, I want that pain to go away. I will make it my job to help him heal. We are a family again and that will help.

To hell with danger, I want him back in our lives permanently.

Suddenly he jumps in his sleep and yells out "NO!" The

noise wakens him and his eyes dart about the room, momentarily disoriented. He looks at me and recognition returns. The clouds clear and he smiles. "My lovely Sam," he says sinking back into the mattress. I squirm a few inches up the bed and kiss him. We share a sweet, gentle kiss. "I love you so much," he sighs.

"I love you too." I kiss him again and without breaking the kiss, I slide my hand off the bandages and downward. As I touch him, he gives a small groan of pleasure and I can feel his urgency.

It sets my body on fire.

55

CAL

Funerals are a time for looking back. As the men in the black suits lower the coffin into the grave, Stammo must be looking back at his role as a father, blaming himself not so much for the things he did but for the things he didn't do. His ex-wife is by his side, sobbing, holding on to Stammo's shoulder, smelling of the gin that she is using to get her through this day in the only way she knows how.

Tyler is here beside a craggy, balding man with a stern face who must be his father. Thanks to Jim Garry, his lawyer, he is out on bail. Garry has told him that he might be facing jail time but maybe, just maybe, not. Tyler must be looking back and wondering at the choices he has made. I am wondering about the choices he might make in the future; it could go either way.

I am looking back to that first meeting with Rebecca Bradbury, a lunch that set this whole thing in motion. As chance would have it, ten days ago she was watching the morning news and saw her husband's murder live. She immediately went into hiding and didn't come out until the news of her daughter's rescue hit the news cycle.

She is a widow and her daughter is fatherless thanks to

the young man being lowered to his final rest. The Bookman. Matt Stammo.

Sam squeezes my right hand. I feel guilty about the bliss of the last seven days. While Stammo has been suffering all sorts of hell, I have been in heaven, for the most part anyway. When the darkness of guilt has descended on me, Sam has been there to help assuage it. She has never asked for details of those last three nights, perhaps she is scared to know; anyway I am grateful for that because I never want her or Ellie to be burdened with the truth about what I have done.

I look at Stammo and see that he is looking at me. I still can't believe that he has forgiven me, except that the essential Stammo is a fair and honest man. His forgiveness means much to me even though it adds an additional barb to my guilt.

The only other people present are Mrs. V., Stammo's land-lady—whose full name I once knew but have forgotten—and a dozen or so cops from the department, some in uniform.

The pastor says some passing words and it is over.

Nick wheels away toward his van, his ex trailing an unsteady path behind him. Everyone respects his obvious need to be alone.

Sam and I turn from the grave and take a couple of steps toward the car park when I hear my name called.

Steve and a uniformed cop have detached themselves from their group. As they approach, I recognize the uniform. He is fresh-faced and red-headed. I had a run in with him a couple of years ago at the scene of my best buddy's murder. He's a little twerp.

As Steve reaches us, I extend my hand but he ignores it. The little twerp smiles.

"Cal," Steve says, "I need you to come with us right now." His face is deadly serious.

"What's this about?" I ask.

"We'll talk about that at Gravely Street." He glances at Sam.

"We'll talk about it right now." I can't keep the aggressive tone out of my voice.

He shrugs. "OK, if that's the way you want it." He glances at Sam again, his face an apology to her. "We processed the crime scene on Samuel Island. We found your blood at the scene and on Matt Stammo's clothing. You can either come with us voluntarily or we will have to place you under arrest here and now for the murders of Carlos Santiago, Edward Perot and Matthew Stammo."

Sam lets go of my hand and takes a stumbling step away from me.

The pain is almost unbearable as I watch that lovely face morph slowly.

From shock.

To horror.

And then to an infinite sadness.

AFTERWORD

Thank you so much for reading Lockstep, my third novel featuring Cal Rogan. If you enjoyed it, I would love it if you could do a review; reviews make a huge difference for an independently published author. You can review it at the website of the retailer from whom you purchased it. Also if you are a member of Goodreads, I would *really* appreciate a review there.

If you have not read *Junkie*, the first Cal Rogan Mystery, I invite you to do so here.

The second book *Oboe* (a real puzzler) is available here.

I will soon be publishing a fourth novel featuring Cal, titled *Three*. If you would like to be part of my launch team and get a free, advanced copy, please go to:

    robertpfrench.com/launchteam

ABOUT THE AUTHOR

Hi. I am a former software developer, turned actor, turned author. The Cal Rogan mysteries are set in Vancouver Canada and, I hope, reflect the best and worst of the city. If you would like to know more about my views on the drug scene, publishing and writing, or would like to contact me:

My website: robertpfrench.com.

Facebook: facebook.com/robertpfrenchauthor

Twitter: @robertpfrench

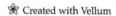

CPSIA information can be obtained
at www.ICGtesting.com
Printed in the USA
LVHW111533160419
614374LV00002B/369/P